Stella the Zombie Kille

STELLA
THE ZOMBIE KILLER
Volume 1

By Alistair Wilkinson

Illustrated by Alison Rasmussen

To Alison, thanks for bringing Stella to life.

TEXT COPYRIGHT: ALISTAIR WILKINSON

ILLUSTRATION COPYRIGHTS: ALISON RASMUSSEN

ISBN: 978-1-326-49673-9

Also by Alistair Wilkinson:

Suspended

Stella the Zombie Killer Volume Two (illustrated by Alison Rasmussen)

For the latest news on Stella the Zombie Killer and other writing visit:

www.alistairwilkinsonauthor.co.uk

Or find Alistair Wilkinson Author on Facebook or tweet @algy04.

To get in touch with Alison Rasmussen tweet @RasmussenAlison.

Acknowledgements

I'm indebted to so many people for helping me to write Stella's adventures. At times I've felt like one of the deads as I tried to push out an episode *every* week! Support and guidance were always needed as were plenty of packets of crisps and mugs of coffee. Publishing an episode every week meant begging, borrowing and stealing people's time for the essential proof reads, so thanks to Lyndsay Bawden and Beth Peck, two work colleagues who have pushed Stella and pushed me to finish each week. My wife Emma for reading the episodes and slapping me every time a character sounds too much like another character and reminding me that there's no point doing it if I rush it. Lucy Adams has read, read and reread, taking the time to correct my words and appreciate the gore. And thank you to everyone who read each and every episode as they came online and for liking and sharing like your hearts depended on it. Some of you I know personally (thank you Penny Ward and Matthew Wilkinson) and there are many more to whom my thanks are sent. You've liked, shared, favourited, retweeted and generally banged that Stella drum. Last but not least, an artist was begged for 'illos'. She responded with creations that have brought Stella and her world to life. Thank you, Alison Rasmussen.

Thank you to you all.

The Cynosure fight for you.

Stella the Zombie Killer Part One

Crash! Stella fell through the ceiling. She leapt up and quickly scanned her surroundings; a kitchen, bare shelves, the floor covered in the debris of searching and looting, empty cupboards, their doors open, and one zombie, a shuffler. Luckily it was on the other side of the room, giving her time to recover from the fall.

The zombie groaned as it shuffled towards her. She looked around but the only option was behind the shambling corpse: a door, a closed door. She didn't know whether it was locked. "But who locks a kitchen door?" she said to the zombie.

It didn't respond.

The kitchen table was between them. It was a simple matter to stand at one end, wait for the zombie to shuffle towards her and then run around the other side. She almost laughed as the dead head jerked around, its lifeless eyes following her movements. On her way past she picked up a carving knife from the table. She gripped the handle securely into the palm of her black, fingerless leather glove.

Reaching the door, Stella pulled the handle. Locked. She rattled desperately but it wouldn't budge. "Who locks a kitchen door!" she said to herself. She looked up; her only way out was back through the ceiling.

Taking a deep breath, she allowed adrenaline to flood her system and then leapt across the table, slid on the shining steel surface and used the momentum to plunge the knife into the zombie's eye. Carrying forward, she slipped off the table and into the zombie, firmly planting her elbow into its chest and knocking it to the floor. She followed it down, landing knees first on the creature's torso, breaking ribs and smashing its skull onto the tiled floor.

Pulling the blade from the socket, she quickly moved to wipe the gore on the back of her combat trousers. The pockets bulged. As she did so she saw something beneath the cabinets on the far side of the room. It glinted faintly in the shadow. She moved carefully towards it, her

movements cautious, as if she thought something would come alive and prevent her from reaching her target.

She laid flat on the floor and reached her arm under the steel cabinet. Dust and grease swiped her finger tips. 'Not gonna pass basic hygiene,' she muttered to herself.

Something ran at her hand and she pulled back in alarm. A rat, its teeth exposed, nose twitching, raised itself in a pugilistic challenge. She batted the creature away and grabbed the object. Pulling it free, she saw that it was a mobile phone, its message light flashing. There was very little dust on its battered but still shiny surface. Someone had dropped it recently.

The screen flared to life at her touch. Immediately she noticed the bars. A signal.

Puzzled, she stared at the phone for a long time, her thumb hovering over the message icon. She pressed it. Password needed. She tutted, the sound echoing in the empty room.

The screen saver was a photograph of a man with a woman. They weren't a couple. Stella knew this instinctively. But the man, tall and angular, his face cruel, looked keen for that to change. The woman was young, blonde and cool, too cool. Her body was relaxed and rigid at the same time, almost as if the side of her furthest away from the man was comfortable and the side near him was trying to solidify into a wall. Stella thought of all the rom-com movie posters she had seen before the crash and how the actors would lean against each other. The woman in the picture was so stiff on one side that she looked she had been photoshopped away from the man, like a rom-com poster torn in half.

Stella wrinkled her nose at the smell pouring out of the zombie. Its eye socket oozed puss and dead brains. 'Gross,' she said out loud as she pocketed the phone and pushed the table under the hole in the ceiling. The noise made by the steel legs scraping along the floor was horrendous. Every zombie in the hotel would hear that, and maybe even an angel as well.

She jumped onto the table and stared up at the hole. She had been down here for at least four minutes; everything could have changed up there and she would be a sitting duck for the few seconds it would take her to climb through the hole.

Waiting an hour would mean that anything that heard the table would have lost interest, but Stella was restless and ready to leave this place. Getting stuck in a hotel was not the plan. Finding Hook and getting some supplies and batteries was the plan. The kitchen was a bust, so she would have to search elsewhere and it was already mid-afternoon. Sunset was at least five hours away. Time was on her side for now as long as she didn't wait around for shufflers to decide to leave.

With the knife clenched between her teeth, she reached up to the hole. Grasping the sides she pulled herself up smoothly, the muscles in her bare arms moving fluidly.

Immediately she knew it was a mistake. Zombies heard her. As her head rose above the hole, she looked around as quickly as she could; four of them. 'Come on then,' she muttered through gritted teeth, the blade of the knife drenched in her saliva. She threw one arm onto the floor, desperately trying to find some purchase. The floor boards she had removed earlier meant that she quickly found a handhold and she was able to hold herself while she threw her other arm up and out of the hole. Heaving herself up to her waist, she spread half of her weight across the floor, leaving just her legs dangling through the hole.

But she wasn't fast enough.

The nearest creature stumbled down to its knees, reaching for her face.

Spitting the knife onto the floor, Stella grabbed the handle and plunged it into the zombie's hand, nailing it to the floor. It looked at her, its dead eyes upset, as if she had offended it in some way. It reached the other towards her.

Quickly she rolled away, kicking the knee of the next creature, making it fold in on itself as if were a toy in the hands of an angry child. Stella was on her feet to face the next and a two-handed shove to its chest sent it sprawling into the wardrobe. The next she allowed to advance at her for half a second before side stepping and pushing it onto the bed. 'Sorry guys, didn't realise you were in here. I'll come back later to clean. Don't forget to tip.'

She headed out of the door, slamming it behind her.

Stella the Zombie Killer Part Two

The windowless hotel corridor was darker than Hook's armpit. Stella wondered where the big man was. They were supposed to meet an hour ago in the lobby but her way had been barred by angels. She had no idea what they were doing in an abandoned hotel in a city ruined by looting and three years of post-apocalyptic hell and she had no intention of finding out. Wherever the angels were was exactly where Stella didn't want to be.

She moved slowly and carefully along the corridor, letting her fingertips slide along the flock wallpaper. It wasn't much of a guide and, not for the first time, she cursed her broken night vision.

Hearing sound ahead, she halted, listening intently while her finger absently traced the flower pattern in the wallpaper. Something was slowly moving towards her, inching its way along the carpeted floor. Definitely along the floor. The sound of dragging had become a soundtrack to Stella's life. So, a whole zombie with broken legs or half a zombie? It didn't really matter; draggers were even easier to deal with than shufflers.

Keeping an ear on the sound, she crept forward. Soon she could make out the creature, a moving lump of shadow, pitiful, even in the dark. Its groaning was more of a desperate wheezing, like a thirsty dog on the edge of death, too tired to even breathe, too broken and useless to even live. Stella kicked her right foot against the skirting board. A blade shot out of the end of her boot, a silver tongue invisible in the dark, but she knew it was there. It was just short enough to allow her to walk freely and just long enough to stab through the nose and into the brain.

She moved to the creature and kicked into its face, shattering the nose and slicing the blade through the skull and into the brain. It was always the brain. Even the angels went down if the brain was destroyed.

Without a backwards glance at the zombie's ruined face, Stella moved forwards to the end of the corridor and the lift doors. She used the metal surface to push the blade back into her boot and then pulled a short jemmy from the deep pockets of her cargo pants. Forcing it between the doors, she slipped her fingers between the gap and pulled them smoothly open.

The shaft was an extension of the darkness but she knew it wasn't very deep. Even so, she decided to risk some light. Producing a torch from her pocket, she flashed it into the space. Cables, thick and grey, the steel glinting in the light, were rod-straight in front of her. Turning the torch's beam down, she could see the bottom of the lift shaft one floor below. That meant the lift itself was above her. She didn't need to know where, so she resisted the temptation to flick the torch upwards.

Switching the torch off, she returned it to her pockets and reached out blindly for the cables, the fingertips of her right hand dancing and waving in the air as she stretched. Leaning a little further, her left hand gripping the edge of the metal door, she finally touched the cable and managed a firm grasp with one hand. Letting go with her left, she swung easily onto the cable and began her short descent.

At the bottom of the shaft, the jemmy was into the crack between the doors and the two panels of metal were pulled smoothly open in just a few seconds. Stella was momentarily blinded by the light flooding through the massive windows in the room beyond. Her eyes quickly adjusted, reducing glare and maintaining optimum vision. She smiled as the tech kicked in. At least something still worked.

The floor to the lobby was waist high and, as far as she could see, empty. She needed to move quickly. Anything with an eye on the lift shaft would have seen the light. Boosting herself, she jumped up and forward, and had her feet firmly on the floor. She immediately set off at a crouched run.

A quick scan of the lobby showed the doors to the street were locked, the carpeted floor was clean, or as clean as could be expected post apocalypse, and the chairs and tables were still neatly arranged, patiently waiting for the guests to take their ease. The place seemed secure.

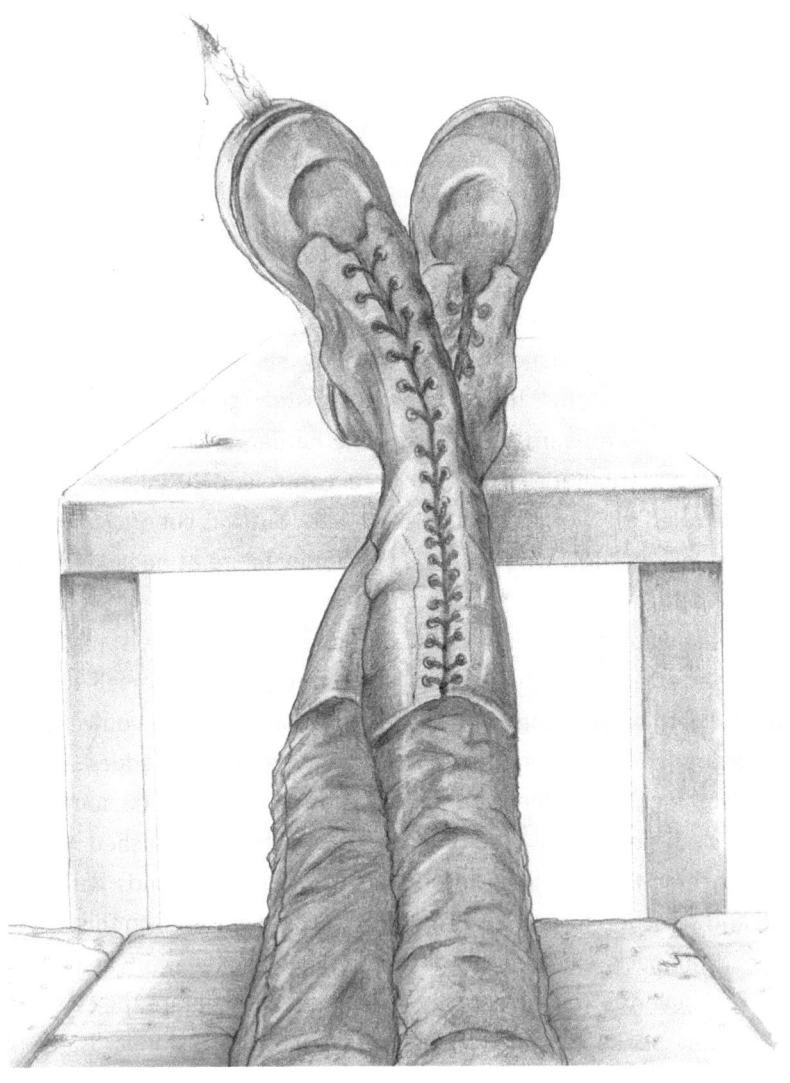

Stella moved to a comfortable arm chair in the corner of the lobby and slowly sat down, sinking into its cushions. She relaxed into the chair, stretching her feet out in front of her, her fat, chunky boots dark blobs in the sunshine as they lolled on the glass coffee table.

From her vantage point she surveyed the space. The room fascinated her. It was so preserved; the windows making it feel like a diorama in a glass case in a museum. She hadn't seen a space like this in years. Dust filled the shafts of sunlight, as the millions of motes raised from her chair turned and moved in a nebular swirl, a galaxy of dead things.

She sat still for long minutes, just staring at the patterns, watching the particles dip and dance and dart. Gently, she blew into the speckles of turning star systems, her light breath casting gentle eddies into the flow. She leaned forward and blew a little harder, creating new patterns and spirals and tributaries here and there, controlling the galaxy.

'If I ruled the world...' she started to say, but was cut off.

'For all we know, you do,' said the burley figure as he landed in the chair opposite her, leaving his back to the room.

Stella watched the universe of particles erupt into the sunlight. She turned her attention to the man, slightly annoyed with herself that she had not heard him coming. 'Hook,' she said. 'Pleased to see you've caught up.' He nodded in mock submission. 'Find anything?' Stella added.

'Nothing. You'd think for such a place there would be something. And check this out.' He waved his arms at the lobby. 'Untouched. Haven't seen anything like this since the crash.' He folded his hands behind his head and slouched further into the chair. 'I could get used to this.' He let his head fall back, exposing his neck. The glint of titanium was obvious. Hook had never bothered keeping his flesh arranged before the crash and the apocalypse had done nothing for his aesthetic standards. 'What would you do anyway?' he said.

Stella wasn't listening. Her attention was on the window directly ahead. Movement.

'What would you do if you ruled the world?' said Hook, still staring at the white ceiling.

'Get down,' said Stella.

'You'd let everyone dance?'

'On the floor!' she hissed.

Hook, recognising the urgency in her voice, was down in a micro second. 'What is it?' he whispered.

'Angels,' said Stella, nodding at the window.

Stella the Zombie Killer Part Three

'Angels!' Jared whispered loudly. He had thrown himself behind a low wall that jutted from the corner of a Tesco store front. The blue and red of the sign were faded and filthy but still recognisable. He cowered there, regretting the decision to come into the city. His group, a ragtag collection of men and women close to starvation, looked to him with fear in their eyes. Fear and something else. Need. They needed him. Ever since the crash they had looked to him to guide them, to protect them. He saw it in their eyes now and the weight of it crushed him. He turned from them and pushed himself against the wall, like he was trying to burrow his way through the bricks and mortar. I can't, he thought to himself. Not this time. I'm sorry, I'm so sorry.

The angels swept overhead, their jet packs roaring to announce their arrival, exhaust trails pale in the heat of a summer's day. The group stopped in a huddle, staring at the floating white figures. Jared peeped from the corner of his eye; three of them, and not so white anymore.

One man, a younger man, one Jared had thought might make it, stepped forward to face them. 'We're just looking for food,' he said to the angels. 'We're not doing anything wrong. No one needs protecting from us. You don't need to arrest us.' The man's voice was clear, just as Jared had heard it a hundred times before. Clear, commanding, even confident if that was still possible. His name was Sean. Jared had gradually given him more and more responsibility, making him an effective second, perhaps more effective than Jared himself. The rest of the group nodded as Sean spoke. Jared could hear a few cries of please added to the man's words. With the angels gripping their complete attention, none of them saw him crouching low against the wall. Slowly, he inched away from his position, careful not to attract attention.

The angels remained silent, hovering above the group, their jet packs whining with the effort. It was the only sound they made. Jared didn't need to see their faces to know it was the only sound they would ever make.

Suddenly, one of them raised their right hand and pointed at Sean. The whole group flinched, looking like they might run. But only for a second. After that they were dead. The angels hosed them with hot, red lasers, burning them where they stood, slicing them in half and slicing on and on even after the bodies had all fallen, their lasers criss-crossing to form a deadly grid that none would escape.

Quickly and silently, Jared fled, tumbling his way across debris-strewn streets. He fell into a doorway when he heard the high pitched whine of the angels' jet packs carrying them away. Shivering, he huddled as far into the space as he could, pulling his knees towards him and burying his head between them to muffle his panicked breathing. He stayed that way for long minutes, trying to calm his breathing so that he could listen.

But it was no use. His breathing was ragged, his heart wouldn't slow.

Up and running again, he fled through the streets, not knowing where he was or where he was going. Desperately he scanned the clear blue skies, looking for the tell-tale contrails of the angels' jet packs. Nothing.

He tripped and fell, skinning his knees badly but rolling straight to his feet.

He stopped. The pain had shocked him into awareness and he paused, scanning the street around him. Nothing but broken glass and abandoned vehicles all covered in the layer of the dust still remaining from the crash. The rains had come after a year of blackness and washed much of it away but here in the cities, there would always be the dust. Beyond the vehicles smashed shop fronts stared at him with dead eyes and silent screaming mouths, like the bewildered victims of a catastrophe.

Falling to his knees, he wretched and choked as bile forced its way up through his larynx, a thin trickle of hot fluid burning his throat and slicing a line along his tongue and drooled from his mouth to form a colourless and pale yellow pile in the dust. His stomach clenched over and over as he dry-heaved, his throat contracting, trying to prevent the hideous but precious fluid from leaving his system. Eventually it stopped, leaving him gasping. He fell onto his side, rolling in the dust and dirt till he lay facing the blue sky.

'I'm sorry,' he said out loud. 'I'm so sorry.'

Dots in the sky. Circling lazily. Three of them. A loose triangle.

Jared stared unblinking, allowing the sun's light to dazzle his eyes. He had to blink away hot tears. Shading his eyes with his hands, he looked towards the dots. They were bigger, moving down. Fast.

He was back on his feet and running in a moment. More carefully this time but still quickly, he dashed to the edge of the street and sprinted along the path. The yawning, broken windows were a blur as he ran.

The scene changed as the shops were replaced with houses, tall five storey town houses. Earls Court, Jared realised. They were just as empty, just as dead. He sprinted on, not knowing where the energy to do so came from, not caring, just pounding his legs till they burned as hotly as his lungs. Anything not to see Sean and the others sliced over and over by the scarlet beams.

Soon he could hear the whine of the jet packs again. Quickly making up his mind, he turned from the town houses and headed back to the shops. A glass-walled hotel, dazzling in the sunshine like a totem from the past, dominated a square surrounded by shop fronts.

Sprinting to the edge of the space, he fell into a smashed shop window, crashing mannequins aside and falling in a heap just inside the shop. He lay covered in the limbs of mannequins, not daring to move and trying to calm his breathing.

Outside, he could see the heat shimmer as the angels' descent brought them closer. Their dirty white metal bodies lowered into view and settled gently on the ground and sending dust dervishes dancing on London's shattered street. Their jet packs powered down, the whining slowing to a soft ticking. Each of the angels stared up at the sky, directly at the sun. Jared could see their faces. They were dead. As dead as the things Jared and his group had been forced to kill so many times. Dead things with the bodies of machines. Each of their right eyes shined a hateful, fading red, the colour gradually dimming to be replaced with a livid blue. Jared had laughed at the early reports of undead cyborgs. He first heard them just after the crash. Impossible, he'd thought. But there they were. Dead men in machines. Dead men who only wanted flesh in machines whose only function was to protect and serve.

They stood in a line facing the sun. Each of the three jet packs cracked open and their wings unfurled. This had been quite a sight before the crash; the angels recharging. Six feet of solar panelling on either side, stretching and curling up above their heads until each angel was surrounded by blazing light. Jared could see the halo. Angels indeed, here to clean this planet.

Stella the Zombie Killer Part Four

'Keep your head down,' Stella whispered at Hook. 'They haven't seen us.'

Hook grunted his reply. They both knew that if the angels had already spotted them then they would already be fighting. Or running. 'How many?' he whispered.

Stella glanced away from the window to Hook. Her nose caught his smell; not rotten exactly, just off. Hook didn't look after his flesh as well as he might. She held up three fingers and waved her hand in the air.

Hook nodded, his face grim: three angels hovering, searching. Although neither he nor Stella had been built for fighting, they had taken care of lone angels when the need arose. Three was another story. He shuffled his bulk to get his head lower behind the comfortable furniture of the lobby. He raised his eyebrows to question Stella.

She shrugged and turned back to the window; the angels were sweeping the area just outside the hotel's entrance. Earl's Court. Stella had been to parties in this area before the crash. Guest of honour. She smirked at the thought now, and then shook her head at Hook who questioned the gesture.

The three suddenly descended and landed just ten metres from the window. They spread themselves apart and then let their wings unfurl. Within seconds the intensity of the golden glow was almost too much.

They're charging,' Stella whispered.

'No way,' Hook replied.

'*Way!*' she said sarcastically.

'They never charge when people are around.'

'They never land when people are around.' she said. Hook nodded in agreement. 'They're either desperate or their scanners are down,' Stella continued, staring through squinted eyes at the blazing golden light. She squinted for the sake of her biological eye; the bionic eyeball had already compensated for the glare.

She turned to Hook and shrugged. She had no idea how the angels were even still functioning. Dead heads in metal bodies. Who was controlling what? 'Something's not right,' she said.

'Not right with them. I say we take them.' Hook was leaning forward against the sofa, his face eager.

'Easy, tiger,' she said, laying a hand on his arm. 'There are three of them.'

'Three of them charging. Three of them offline.'

'Do they shut down fully?'

Hook nodded.

Stella smelled his breath and grimaced.

He smiled at her and cocked his head to one side. He was a good looking man. 'We just walk up to them and knock their blocks off. Easy.'

Stella glanced back outside, the golden shine full on the lobby's expansive windows. 'I don't know. Seems too easy. Even if we take out the dead heads doesn't mean the suits won't kick off. There's no way they would let their defences down.'

'They're fried. They don't know where they are. Dead heads must have controlled the suits and now they're acting on impulse. They needed recharging so they're recharging. Dead heads don't think. Dead head angels don't think.' Hook looked at her, his face suddenly serious. 'And we could really use those suits.'

Stella remembered her broken night vision. 'Okay,' she nodded. 'We take them. But the second it goes wrong I'm out of there. Understood?'

Hook grinned. 'You know me, Stella. Understand is my middle name. What's the plan?'

'Nothing complicated. You take the one on the left, I take the one on the right. If the third wakes up we get the hell out of there. That's it. If it doesn't,' she shrugged, 'we knock its block off.'

'Ready when you are, boss.'

'I'm no one's boss, Hook. Stop calling me that.'

He winked. 'You know I like to be told what to do.'

Stella looked over the back of the couch. The three of them were still there, still standing stock still, still surrounded in that golden glow. She was jealous of the solar power. Her own augments were mostly defunct because they needed constant charging either from high energy food or an external power supply. Neither were readily available anymore, which had led to a reliance on less subtle means to keep her operating at anything close to full capacity. For a moment she wondered whether it would be possible to use the angels' solar panelling. Gregor was good but she didn't think even he could handle a full mod and rebuild, not with the tools available.

'Hey?' said Hook, clicking his fingers and stirring her from her thoughts. 'We ready?'

'Don't do that,' said Stella, jerking her head back away from his fingers. 'It's rude.'

'Manners were burned in the crash, boss. Now it's just do or don't and we're ready to do. C'mon, let's go.'

Stella nodded. 'We need to be quick. Make a way through for us, then go left. Meet you in the middle.'

Hook grinned as they leapt over the sofa and dashed to the lobby doors, Stella right behind him. She was faster than Hook but he was better than her at making holes.

Hook grabbed a thick cushion on the way past and raised his arms in front of his face, cushion to the front, and ran with firm, heavy-footed strides at the doors, crashing through the toughened safety glass, lacerating the cushion and drawing some blood on the bare skin of his forearms.

Glass showered onto the path outside, raining on Stella as she followed Hook's bulk through the shattered doorway.

She headed right, quickly outpacing Hook. The three angels, golden wings spread and arched over their heads, stood still as if waiting for the assault. She leapt at the angel on the right, bowling it over and wrapping her legs around its torso, crushing the fragile solar panels. Half a second later she was on the ground with the inert machine-thing held securely in place, its wings spilling out either side like ragged golden sheets. She grabbed its head, pulling and twisting, ignoring its one dead eye, which was even yellower in its golden glow and skilfully kept her fingers under its chin, away from the biting teeth. The head was loose and flaccid but its neck, half flesh, half wires and cables, held firm at first. Grunting, she twisted sharply and heaved at the head, breaking its neck with a loud crack. Her thin, sharp fingers pushed and forced their way through the rotten flesh around its chin. Ignoring the feeling of putrescence under her nails she pulled as hard as she could, her knees forcing the torso away from the head. She saw the blue bionic eye flash red and redoubled her efforts, straining against the sinew and metal holding the head in place. Finally she felt the first snapping of cords and cables, quickly followed by the tear of skin and rush of rotten gore as its head was pulled from its shoulders.

She rolled away, detangling her legs from the angel in an instant, and looked over to see Hook already heading for the middle angel. She leapt to her feet to rush to meet him, the hair of the angel's head wrapped in her fingers.

But they were too slow.

The remaining angel faced Hook. Its wings were gone and its arm was up and pointing directly at him.

The big man fell to the floor in the instant that the red beam swept the air where his chest had been a split second before.

'We run!' Stella shouted as she turned away from the angel and sprinted back to the hotel lobby. The lift shaft would provide effective cover from an angel with broken scanners.

Crunching through the doorway, she leapt over the first sofa, using its bulk to shield her as she risked a glance backwards. The angel was not following her.

Pausing, she crouched low to keep the sofa between her and the outside world. With the golden glow gone, the summer sunshine seemed weak, washed out. But she could see the angel. It was stalking its prey, walking slowly away from her.

She scanned the area for Hook but she couldn't see him; her view was restricted and she didn't dare to reveal herself to get a better look. 'Damn,' she whispered to herself. 'Where the hell are you?'

The angel was about to move out of her sight. 'Do or don't,' she said quietly and stood up to look.

Hook was charging the angel.

'What the hell?' said Stella and then repeated herself more loudly. 'What the hell!'

The angel raised its arm. Stella waited for the flash of red, for Hook to be sliced neatly in two. It didn't happen and the big man slammed into the angel, sending it and him sprawling into the dust.

Stella made her decision. She tapped her foot against the leg of the sofa, sending the blade out of the end of her right boot, and sprinted for the melee. She covered the ground in under two seconds. 'Up and push!' she shouted to Hook.

His face straining, Hook grabbed the angel and hauled it upright, pushing it into the air and holding it as high as he could.

Stella hit the kerb, leapt, spun in the air and brought her right boot around and into the side of the creature's head, breaking its neck and stabbing the life from its brain.

Hook threw the angel to the floor and stamped on the mechanical half of its head. He looked to Stella. His face was shining and he was breathing hard. 'Nice kick, boss.'

'*Understand* is your middle name?'

He grinned. 'I understood.' He tapped the side of his head and gently kicked the angel's arm. 'Only enough recharge for one shot.'

'And how did you find that out?'

Hook laughed. 'I didn't die when it tried to shoot me again.'

Stella the Zombie Killer Part Five

Stella hefted the headless body of the angel onto her back. Its metal components grated uncomfortably across her shoulders and the smell of its rotting corpse was disgusting. The head dangled from her belt, the leather looped through its mouth making it leer up at her. 'Easy there, fella. Not on a first date,' she said to it.

'You what?' said Hook. He had an angel over each shoulder and was smiling broadly, happy with the day's catch. He stood on top of a car bonnet, scanning the street. His weight pushed the vehicle's front end down towards the debris strewn, filthy ground.

'Nothing.' She stared at Hook's crotch. His legs were parted, braced against the weight on his shoulders and through them she could see a broken shop window, scattered mannequins...

Hook's smile disappeared when he saw the look on Stella's face. He raised his eyebrows.

Stella nodded behind him. Movement, she mouthed to him, silently. She placed her angel carefully onto the floor. 'Just need to check the lobby one last time,' she said. 'I'm sure I saw some food in that back office.'

Hook nodded. 'Take your time. The thumpers are still up and running; we'll be safe for hours.' He dropped the angels from his shoulders, letting them slam and slide from the car's bonnet. The car rocked and rolled as he stepped down.

Stella glanced back on her walk to the hotel lobby to see Hook hoist his foot onto the bonnet of the car and bend to his shoe laces. His massive frame looked slightly ridiculous competing such a mundane task.

Entering the lobby, she ducked down, sure that the debris in the street would cover her, and scampered back out of the smashed doorway, switched left, crouch-ran for fifty yards and dashed across the street. On the opposite path she straightened and trotted towards the broken shop window opposite Hook, who was still investigating his shoe laces. He was never one for subtlety, she thought to herself.

The shop window was just a few yards ahead. Glass crunched as she covered the distance in two seconds.

Hook, matching her approach, dropped his foot and ran at the window.

They both burst through into the shop, scattering the mannequins and surprising the man cowering amongst the plastic limbs. Feebly, he held his arms over his head, remaining silent, just waiting.

Stella had stopped and held her arm out to halt Hook as soon as she saw him. The man was pathetic, no threat. She stared down at him, watching him try to push himself away, scraping his worn out shoes against the broken glass and mannequins. The dust and filth from the crash was still thick in here; the building itself sheltering the shop from the rains. Stella glared at him and realised that he had nothing left. 'Who are you?' she said.

The man stopped his futile efforts and slowly lowered his arms just enough to peer over them. 'Jared,' he said. 'Jared Jenks.' His voice was tired, defeated.

'Sounds like a superhero alter ego,' said Hook. 'You got a mask in your pants?'

Jared looked to the big man, confusion and terror in his eyes.

'Don't worry about him,' said Stella. The man on the ground was older than her, mid-forties at least and possibly even older at first glance. That could be his condition, Stella thought. Half-starved and exhausted did nothing for the complexion.

Jared stared at her. 'You're her,' he said, his eyes widening in recognition. 'You're The Killer.'

Stella grunted a laugh. 'Not for a long time, Mr Jenks,' she said. 'My days of killing in the ring are over.'

'You were the Cynosure three years running. Every year up to the crash. My eldest boy had posters of you.'

'I'll bet he did,' Hook smirked.

Stella elbowed him. 'Not the right time, meathead,' she said and then turned to Jared. 'Can you stand up?'

Jared nodded and tried to stand. He could barely lift himself from the floor.

'Looks like you're all partied out, Jared Jenks,' said Stella, smiling at the man. She didn't move to help him. 'What are you doing out here alone, anyway? We haven't seen a live one for months.'

'We came into the city to find food. There's nothing left. We were starving.'

'"We?",' said Stella. 'You lost your group?'

Jared coloured, nodded, said nothing.

Stella looked to Hook, who looked back at her, shrugged. Stella nodded.

Hook sighed a little. 'Looks like you won the lottery, little man,' he said to Jared, before turning to Stella. 'What about the angels?'

'You take your two and I'll come back for the other one. I'll help Mr Jenks.' She bent to Jared. 'I just need to see your wrists and ankles, Mr Jenks. Just to check, you understand.' She pulled his sleeves back and then his trouser hems. Finding nothing, she grunted in satisfaction.

'Got any batteries, JJ? You need batteries to get into our place,' said Hook.

'Ignore him,' said Stella, smiling reassuringly and helping Jared to his feet. 'We've got a place you can stay. Not exactly comfortable, but safe.' She looked at him thoughtfully and added, 'You don't have any batteries do you?'

'No, sorry,' Jared replied.

'Never mind,' said Stella.

'Where are we going?' Jared's head lolled on Stella's shoulder.

'Easy,' said Stella. 'I need a little help, Mr Jenks. You're a dead weight.'

'Pun intended?' Jared slurred.

Stella laughed grimly. 'Possibly. We'll see.'

'Where are we going?' Jared repeated.

Hook caught up with them. 'Vic's,' he said, but Jared had closed his eyes.

Stella sighed, crouched, let Jared flop over her and hoisted him across her shoulders. 'He smells nearly as bad as you,' she said.

'But he ain't as good looking,' Hook replied, grinning at her.

They walked on east through the streets of a devastated London. Limp litter flopped in their path. It was shifted by the light breeze so that it raised itself feebly and then gave up, dying each time a whiff of wind gave it some semblance of life. Faded graffiti covered the walls and told of terror and death and warned against entry, as if warnings were needed. The redundancy of the messages had always pained Stella. Right from the crash the words had been daubed and the people had died and died and died, regardless of warnings. The words continued on the abandoned cars. They slumped with their tyres flat, doors and fuel caps open and inviting but leading to nothing, the vehicles just empty shells, metal and glass frames drained of their fuel, their owners dead and still walking.

The silence was broken by a soft but insistent alarm. Stella glanced down at her pocket. 'Thumper's out.'

Hook nodded. 'We're nearly home. Should be fine.'

Stella reached her hand to her bleeping pocket, easily balancing Jared as she did it, and turned the alarm off. She glanced skyward at the distant sound of jet packs.

'Long way away,' said Hook.

Stella nodded in reply but they both moved closer to the buildings, as far away from the middle of the street as they could.

Smashed glass was ground against the pavement by the soles of their boots, its cracking protests so old and familiar they went unheeded. They trudged along West Cromwell Road, past a smashed Tesco and the ghostly Point West Apartments, its dark windows, filled with whispered threats, glowering at them as they moved beneath its shadow. Stella quickened her steps, Hook moving smoothly beside her, kept pace comfortably. 'I hate that place,' said Stella.

'Creepy,' Hook agreed. 'We keeping this one?' He nodded at Jared.

'He's not a pet. It'll be up to him.'

'Just looking out for you, boss. I know how you get upset when they, well, you know.'

'Leave it, Hook.' Stella's voice carried a warning which Hook heard and ignored.

'You can't save everyone, Stella.'

'Never tried to.' Grim faced, she walked ahead, ignoring the big man.

Hook sighed dramatically and followed behind, allowing the distance between them to increase. 'C'mon, Stella, I didn't mean anything by it.'

Stella ignored him.

They walked on in silence, only stopping when they reached the Victoria and Albert Museum.

The grand entrance towered over them, the two solid wooden doors, dark and weathered, waited for them at the top of a short flight of steps.

'Home sweet home,' said Hook. 'Hope Gregor's got the kettle on.' He looked to Stella, smiling between the backsides of the two angels over his shoulders.

Ignoring him, Stella climbed the steps and banged a complicated rhythm on the left door. She waited ten seconds and repeated the rhythm.

The door swung open to reveal a stocky man, grey-haired, middle fifties, suspicious eyes scanning Stella and Hook, flicking his gaze between the bodies of the angels and then the prone figure of Jared. 'What's that?' he said pointing to Jared. His fingers were almost black with dirt and oil.

'And hello to you too, Gregor. Nice to see that you're safe and nothing's eaten you while we've been gone,' said Stella. She shook her head theatrically at him. 'This is Mr Jenks,' she continued. 'I think he could use our help.'

Gregor scowled. 'Anyone still walking and talking at the same time needs our help. Can't bring them all in.'

'We can bring in the ones we find,' Stella said sharply.

Gregor shrugged and stepped aside. He nodded at Hook as the big man passed inside and then, with a searching look of the street, pulled the heavy door closed and lowered a thick wooden bar into place. The other door was similarly braced.

They hauled their loads through the initial entrance, past toilets and cloakrooms surrounded by grand pillars. Through more pillars they emerged into the rotunda. A large ringed desk dominated the room. The space inside it was taken up with work benches and machinery. Above that a huge chandelier made of spirals of dusty green and blue glass that sparkled in the summer afternoon sun. Three large sunlit avenues stretched away from the rotunda.

Hook bustled through to the work benches, slapping the angels' corpses down one by one. 'A bit of salvage for you, Gregor. Should be of some use.'

Gregor moved to the benches, nodding his head. 'I'll have these stripped down by nightfall. Get the buckets ready.'

'Let me guess, my turn for slopping out?' said Hook to Stella. He sighed as she nodded to him while she laid Jared carefully on the remaining work bench.

'Did you get batteries?' said Gregor.

They both shook their heads. 'Got this though,' said Stella fishing the phone from her pocket. 'It's got a signal.' She threw it to Gregor.

He studied the screen.

'It's password protected,' said Stella.

'Where'd you get that?' said Hook. 'You never told me.'

Stella shrugged. 'Forgot about till now.'

Gregor concentrated on the screen. 'Shouldn't be a signal. Nothing to give it one. All the satellites came down in the crash.'

'All of them?' said Stella. 'How can you be sure?'

'I can't,' Gregor replied. 'Just assuming.' He stared thoughtfully at the screen. 'There must be operational masts for this thing to work. We need to find them.'

'I'll go tomorrow,' said Stella.

Stella the Zombie Killer Part Six

Gregor got to work on the angels lying on his tables. He methodically cut away flesh, sawing and slicing and filling bucket after bucket with lumps of rotten gore.

'You get the best jobs,' said Hook, lifting two huge buckets of grey meat at once.

Gregor just grunted.

Stella was lifting Jared onto her shoulders. 'I'm gonna take Mr Jenks somewhere more comfortable,' she said.

'You mean a rolled up mat on the floor?' said Hook. 'He'd be better where he is.'

'Let's just say I wouldn't want Gregor's tools to slip and accidently fall on him.' She smiled as she said it.

'We can't feed everyone,' Gregor growled, his head bent towards his gruesome task. Sweat covered his forehead and, on the rare occasions he glanced up from his work, it shone in the late afternoon sunlight.

Hook lugged his load down the east corridor.

'Remember to check nothing's around before you tip that out,' said Stella.

'Uh huh,' the big man called over his shoulder.

Stella moved north and into the gift shop, converted now to a bedroom of sorts. She had filled the shelves with books scavenged on her various trips into the city. Other than that, there was a sleeping mat and a chair. Patterned throws hung at the windows and the door, which she closed, plunging the room into a gloomy shade. Not much, but it was the closest thing she had to a private space.

She didn't know why she brought Jared in here; if he was awake, he certainly wouldn't be welcome. She sighed as she laid him down on her mat. 'Sleep well, Mr Jenks.' She settled in the chair and grabbed a book from the shelves and clicked on a reading lamp. 'The Road' by Cormac

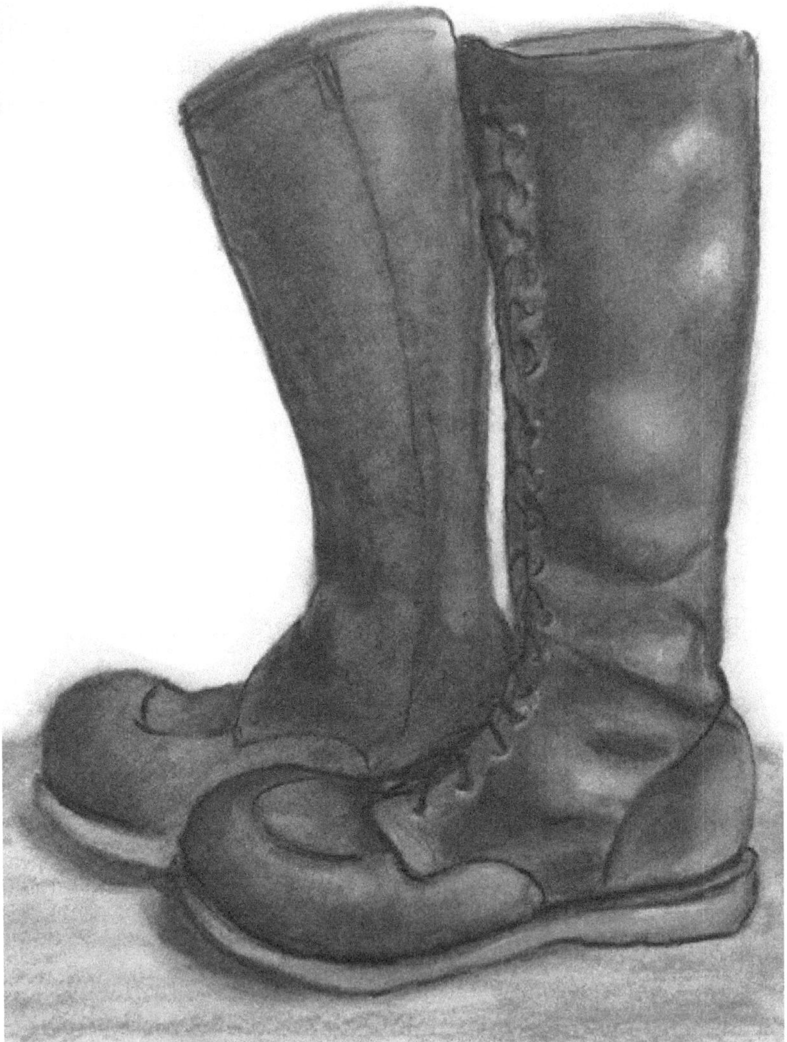

McCarthy. 'A little bit of non-fiction,' she said to herself, and settled to read.

Stella jerked awake. Someone was standing over her. She lashed out with her fist, connecting with someone's jaw. The figure yelped and fell over. Stella was up, out of the chair and standing over him in an instant, ready to press her attack.

Jared covered his head with his arms. 'I'm sorry, I'm sorry, I'm sorry,' he said.

Stella stopped, reached her hand down to him. 'It's okay,' she said, with never a thought of an apology. 'I should warn you, I don't like to be woken up. If you ever need to do it again, you should do it from a distance.'

Jared reached for her hand and allowed himself to be pulled smoothly to his feet. His jaw was already red and starting to swell. 'Noted,' he said.

Stella stared at him.

He flinched again.

'Don't be nervous. You're not in danger here,' said Stella.

'We're in danger everywhere,' said Jared.

Stella nodded. 'You must be hungry.' She looked at his drawn face, his sunken eyes. 'Breakfast.'

She led him from the gift shop back to the rotunda, where Gregor and Hook were already up and eating.

'Morning, JJ,' said Hook. He saw the blossoming bruise on Jared's face. 'Rough night?' He winked at Stella, who ignored him.

Gregor glared at Jared. Both he and Hook ate from bowls, spooning what looked and smelled like baked beans into their mouths.

'Sit here,' said Stella, pointing to a stool on the outside of the ringed desk. She walked into the middle and met him on the other side of the black wood. 'We have just what a starving man needs.' She placed a tin of baked beans and sausages in front of Jared.

He stared at it, open mouthed.

Hook laughed.

Stella smiled. 'Hot or cold?' she said.

Jared looked at her. 'How will you heat it? Might get a bit smoky in here if you light a fire.'

Hook and Stella laughed, even Gregor smirked. 'No problem,' said Stella. She took the tin, opened it with a tin opener and poured the contents into a bowl. She reached below the counter and Jared heard a series of old but familiar sounds: a door opening, buttons pressed and the whir of a microwave oven.

His mouth dropped open again. 'You've got power?'

Stella smiled. 'Solar. A little present from our almost-visitors. Vic's was one of the first places to be kitted out with the new gear.'

'No problems with it?' said Jared.

'Nothing serious so far,' said Gregor.

'We've had to steal a few parts from places,' said Hook, smiling. 'Some of the streetlights don't work anymore.'

'It's not stealing, not anymore' said Jared. 'No one to steal it from.' His haggard face was glum again. 'Wait a minute,' he said. 'You have working streetlights?'

The other three nodded. Jared managed to look even glummer. 'I've not seen a working streetlight for years.'

'Cheer up and eat up,' said Stella, placing a steaming bowl in front of him.

'So, what's the plan?' said Hook. Breakfast was finished. Gregor was already busying himself at his now gore-free work stations, Hook had taken the pots away, Stella was waiting calmly and Jared was still too stunned to speak.

'We track down a working mobile phone mast,' said Gregor, speaking from behind the mechanical parts of the angels stacked on his table. 'It should give us an idea of how this phone is working, what bandwidth is being used. It might even give us some idea about where the signals are coming from.

'That's my job,' said Stella. 'Where do I start?'

Gregor shrugged. 'Tall buildings have them stashed away inside their roofs. Plenty of those to choose from.'

'What about this place?' said Jared.

'We've cleaned it out,' said Gregor, spreading his arms to take in the whole building. 'Top to bottom. Anything techy is already down here. And I don't remember a mobile mast.'

'Next door then,' said Stella. 'Front of the Natural History's tall enough and if there wasn't one in here, good chance there's one in there.'

'Not exactly a clear logic,' said Gregor. 'But close enough.'

'And we won't need thumpers, so we save a few batteries,' said Stella.

'What are thumpers?' asked Jared.

'Ultra sound,' said Gregor. 'You've heard of the Mosquito devices they put in shops to clear teenagers?' Jared nodded. 'Similar to those. We set up a thumper and it broadcasts an ultra-sonic rhythm, like a beat that we can't hear. Sends the zombies crazy; they can't get enough. Drawn to it like moths to a flame.'

'Why call it a thumper?' said Jared.

'Because it thumps into their ears and brains. Duh, duh, duh!' said Hook, banging the desk.

'That's where all the deads are,' said Jared.

The other three nodded. 'Zombie catnip,' said Hook.

'Is that what you call them?' said Stella. 'Deads?'

'Yeah. Not very imaginative.'

'Spot on though,' she replied. She turned to Hook. 'I'm gonna take this one alone, okay?'

'Not a problem,' he replied. 'I was never one for sneaking about. And the garden needs a bit of TLC. I'll sort that and we can all have a freshly cooked meal tonight.'

Jared stared from one to other, bemused. 'It's not like this where I came from.'

Before she left the safety of Vic's, Stella went upstairs to check the streets. She leant over a harpoon launcher to look out of the arched windows onto the street outside. The trees on the other side of the road were overgrown, unchecked; Stella could barely see the red phone box against the rampant green. The Ismaili Building stood silent and empty, its windows still covered in the filthy fallout from the crash. Ignoring it all, she checked for zombies. The streets were mostly clear, just a few shufflers, deads, she corrected herself, on the road but that was to be expected; a handful always drifted once the thumpers' signals were cut. Satisfied, she moved swiftly down the stairs, through the rotunda, past the cloakrooms and out of the door, closing it softly behind her.

One of the deads sensed her immediately. How some of them seemed to be aware while others spent days walking into a glass wall like fat, drunken flies, she had never figured out. She touched the sheathed knife strapped to her leg. A weapon wasn't always best; a sword was too big, a club too cumbersome, but the tanto, a Japanese dagger with a twelve inch blade, was small enough to fit between hip and knee so as not obstruct movement. She knew that not taking it on her last outing was a sign of something. She didn't want to think what. Glancing down at the blade, she smiled. It was from one of Vic's displays when they had first arrived after the crash. Stella had looked after it well, cleaning and sharpening it almost daily.

From across the street, the dead stumbled towards her, its initial jerky movements lying to give it the illusion of speed. Stella knew that it would be a minute before it made it to her position. She decided to ignore it and headed for the Natural History Museum.

The front doors, almost hidden amongst the wild trees and shrubs that grew out of control in front of the museum, were at the top of three short flights of hand-railed steps. They were barricaded. Over a year ago she and Hook had made sure that anything inside couldn't get outside to come bother them. 'So,' she said to herself, 'when you close the door *before* the horse has bolted, how do you get back in?'

She stood and stared at the two enormous towers that flanked the main entrance. If there were masts, they would surely be at the top of those towers. There were huge arched windows at the bottom of each tower which she could easily break, but she hesitated, knowing that that would leave a permanent hole in the front of the museum. A permanent hole that could leak deads. She didn't fancy clearing the whole building. 'Maybe that's a job for Hook,' she said aloud.

She sighed and allowed her shoulders to slump. 'What to do, what to do...'

Her hand moved quickly to the tanto as she whirled around and the blade was out of its sheath and into the top of the dead's head in the blink of an eye. It was the same one that had seen her leaving Vic's. Stella stared at it for the brief second that it stayed upright. The tip of her blade poked beneath its chin, blood dripping from the end. She looked closer at its face. Its eyes never changed. None of them ever did. Dead before, dead now. Nothing left, there was no release. No soul.

She gripped the handle and pulled as it fell. The knife came free. The dead's raggedy clothes were used to wipe the tanto clean before it was replaced in its sheath.

'Well, Hook could use the exercise,' she said to the limp corpse. She walked forward, and with one massive boot, kicked a metal strut holding the hand rail, stooped for the rail, twisted and snapped it away from the strut and stalked towards the window on the right. 'I think I'll go through the arched window today,' she said as she raised the bar high.

She brought it down, sword-like, through the glass, shattering the entire two-and-a-half metre pane. Once the glass had stopped falling and the appalling noise had settled, she looked through into the room beyond. Three deads were already shuffling their way towards the broken remains of the frame.

'Hi honeys, I'm home,' she said as she leapt through the gap.

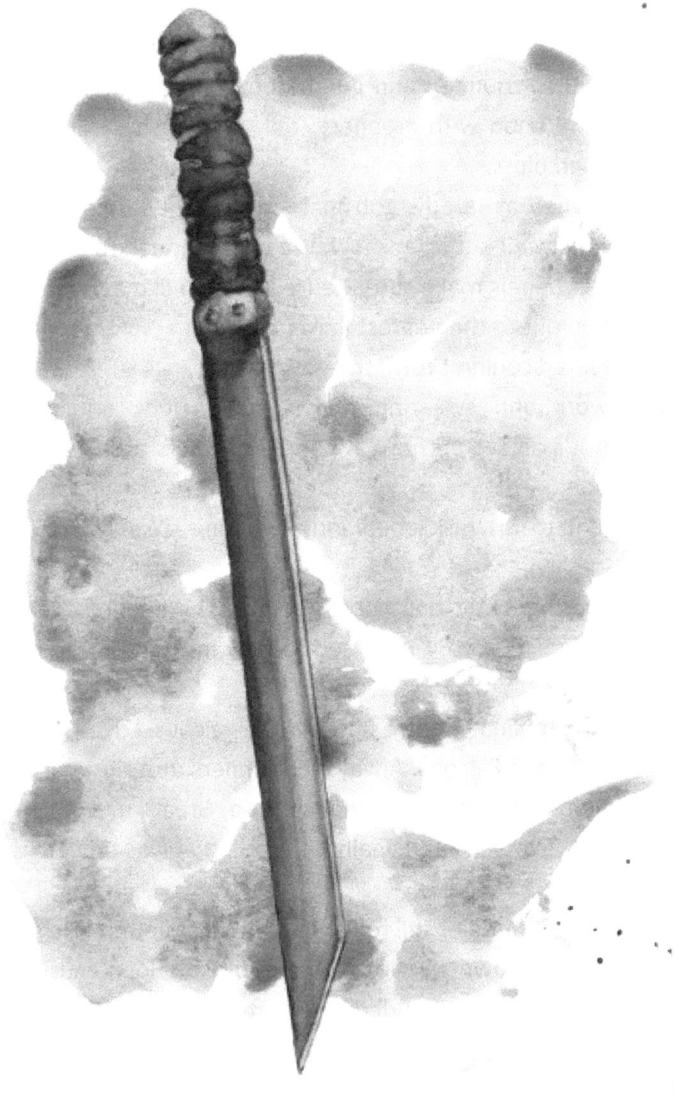

Stella the Zombie Killer Part Seven

Jared had followed Hook outside into the garden. The space was glorious; a square of land surrounded and guarded by the tall, white buildings of the museum and filled with greenery; tall, low, bushy, skinny plants in ordered rows and plots.

Hook laughed at Jared's gobsmacked face. 'It's taken a while but we're pretty much self-sufficient now. We grow enough to last us all year round. The solar panels make sure the freezers run like a dream. Hell of a job lugging them out of the nearest Iceland though.'

'How...' Jared couldn't form the words.

'Hard work and swearing mainly,' said Hook anticipating the question. 'But it's all set up now. A couple of hours a day should see it right. Grab a hoe.'

Jared bent to his task obediently, working steadily under Hook's direction.

Jared's permanently bent posture made him seem even smaller than the large-framed Hook. 'You used to play in the Games,' he said. It wasn't a question.

'Yep,' Hook replied. 'Centre back for the Falcons. Loved it.'

'I remember the Falcons. Always the runners up.'

'Yeah, we never quite made that step up. Great guys though. Great guys, great times.' Hook leaned against a spade that was tiny in his hands. 'Were you a fan?'

'My kids,' said Jared. 'I still followed football. Chelsea.' He shrugged.

'I was turned down by Nottingham Forest,' Hook mused. 'I was gutted, thought my life had ended.' He tutted at himself. 'Didn't know what the end looked like then.' He straightened his back and sighed. 'Then the Message came and everything changed. Everything was gonna be fantastic. Nottingham Forest didn't matter anymore and when they came up with the idea for the Cynosure Games I jumped at the chance. Six months of mods,' he flexed his arms and chest, making his muscles ripple with brutal, augmented strength. 'Five years of competing and still not a problem with them.'

'Still got the hook?'

'Yep.' Hook shot out his arm, curling it round an imaginary opponent. 'Hook 'em in, bring 'em down. That was me,' he said proudly.

Movement caught Jared's eye and he jerked his head around.

'Easy, JJ,' said Hook. 'You're safe in here.'

Jared peered at a section separated by a wire mesh fence. 'Chickens?' he said. Two birds pecking at the dirt and more joining them.

Hook nodded. 'They're Stella's job. I can't stand cleaning them out.'

'How many?'

Hook shrugged. 'Couple of dozen. She looks after them well. But then she does everything well.'

Jared nodded. 'She's the Cynosure,' he whispered.

The pole was a blur in Stella's hands as she smacked the three deads on their arms and shoulders, sending them tottering around the room, bumping into each other, against furniture, falling and trying to regain their footing. 'C'mon guys, you can dance harder than that. Pick up the pace!' She moved with a grace and speed that would have made live people look clumsy, so the deads were like scarecrows on strings and Stella pulled and pushed them, even risking a shove with her hands. She was glad of her black fingerless gloves but her fingertips pressed hard into their clothing and she could feel the rotten flesh yielding to the bone beneath.

An ancient computer monitor stood at the corner of a desk. 'Well,' said Stella to the deads, 'I know this is a museum, but that's even deader than you.' She span away and blew the dust out of the plastic ribs at the back of the monitor. 'If we could just teach you guys to clean...' She smacked the nearest dead on the nose, jabbing into its face, breaking skin and bone. She boxed the creature's face, laughing loudly as its head jerked back and forth, its wispy hair dancing to the blows.

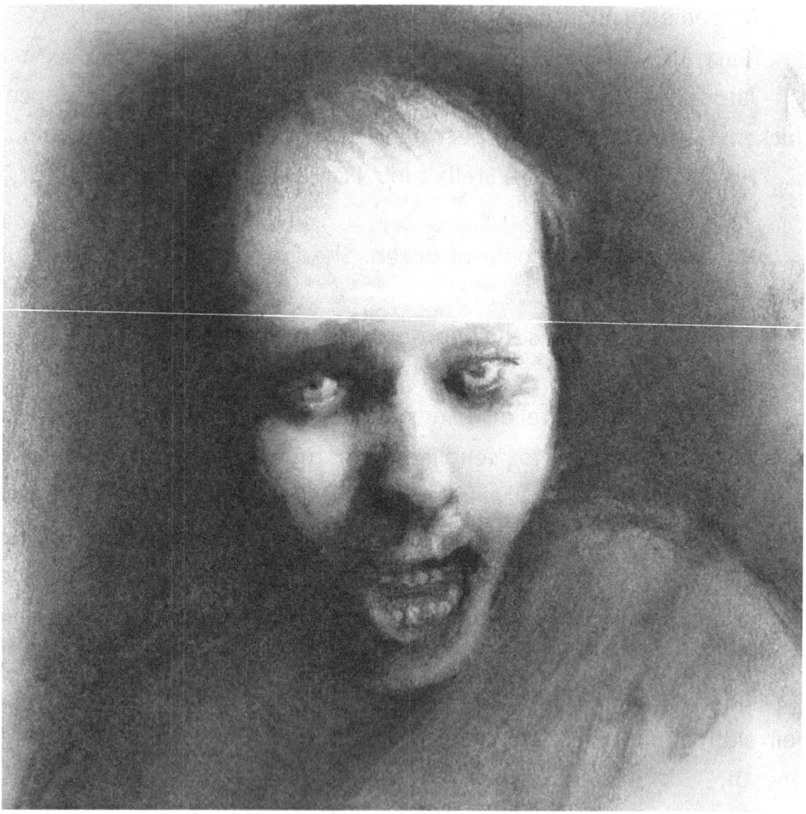

'What do you think?' she said to it. 'Can I get away with a do-si-do?' The dead stared at her, its bloody face slack, drool dripping from its mouth, its yellow eyes unresponsive. Stella dropped the pole and lurched at it, grabbed its wrists, cracking the bones beneath the thin veil of skin, and spun it around so quickly it couldn't attack her properly, managing only to thrust its face forward and champ its teeth uselessly. Stella laughed at it and used it to bat the other two out of the way. 'Yee-ha!' she yelled, spinning faster before finally letting go, sending the dead sprawling against a desk, crashing it and its contents, bulky monitor included, to the floor.

'I don't suppose you ever need to worry about her?' said Jared.

'No need,' Hook replied. 'Like you say, she's the Cynosure.' Jared noticed that this last was said without Hook's usual enthusiasm. He saw Jared's expression. 'I guess I'm just jealous,' he explained. 'I never got to win.'

'You're winning now.' Jared raised his arms to take in the garden.

'Yeah,' Hook smiled. 'I've got my uses.'

'Have you two been together since the crash?'

'Yeah. There was a tournament. The Falcons were already out but the Mariners, Stella's team, they were going all the way as usual.'

'I remember. It was on the TV. She scored more points that night than she ever had before. It was gonna be her year. Again.'

'I hung around to watch,' Hook added, slightly sheepishly, Jared thought. 'You know, just to be part of it. Wembley Stadium. One hundred and ten thousand people all chanting her name. It was history and I wanted to be there.'

Jared watched the big man talk. The memories filled him, making his face shine with colour, like he was remembering a dessert trolley. 'You never managed to hook Stella, did you?' Jared asked.

'No chance.' Hook laughed. 'She was too quick for me.' He glanced at over the roofs in the direction of the Natural History Museum. 'Still is,' he added.

'She always goes out alone?'

'A lot of the time. We go together when she's already scouted an area or planted the thumpers. She's a bit more subtle than me.'

'Woah! Head rush. Settle down, guys. We're just getting started. Plenty of time.' Stella wiped her brow and stooped for the pole. Spinning it casually, she walked to the prone zombie. It raised its head as she approached and dragged its feet into itself, preparing to try to stand.

She brought the pole around in a blurred arc smashing one and then two kneecaps. The dead fell back on itself and Stella turned to the next one. She charged it, pole horizontal like a lance and skewered the dead in the stomach, pushing it back against the wall, smashing shelves and sending their contents tumbling to the floor. Momentum carried the pole through the dead's stomach and into the wall behind. It thudded into the plaster, knocking a hole in the wall.

Stella pulled out the pole and span it above her head as she turned to the last dead standing. 'I think that that's just about it and my card's already marked for later. So I'm afraid you'll have to sit this one out.' She let the pole slide through her gloved palms till she held it in a two-handed grip. Swinging it head height, she connected with the side of the dead's head and, such was the force of the blow, its skull collapsed and the bar travelled through into its brain.

'Gross,' she said and, without looking, buried the end of the bar into the head of the dead slumped at the base of the wall.

The one with the broken knees was using its arms to crawl to her. She shook her head at its efforts as she stooped for the monitor. 'Who said old tech is useless?' she said as she dropped it onto the dead's head. Its crushed skull spewed blood and brain matter over the floor, making her skip to the side to avoid it. 'Watch it. These boots don't grow on trees.'

Glancing up, she saw the door to the rest of museum start to budge. 'About time,' she said as the face of another dead peered around the door. 'Do you know how long I've been waiting?'

She turned and moved to the broken window and the glaring daylight. 'Laters,' she sang to the dead and jumped back out to the front of the Natural History Museum, leaned against the wall and propped her foot casually against the bricks.

'What about you, JJ? What did you do before the crash?' said Hook.

Jared started to correct the other man on his name, but he left it. It was nice to have a new identity. 'Army,' he said. 'Right up until the Disbandment. I was career military. Made it to captain, was ready to go all the way.'

'Captain Jenks, eh?' said Hook approvingly.

'Not sure I could have cut it though. Not with what's happened since.'

'You're still alive,' Hook pointed out.

'Yeah,' Jared nodded, 'I'm still alive.'

'What did you do after the army? I heard a lot of them volunteered for the angels.'

'You heard right. I was in Angel Control, overseeing deployment and the first beats. It was successful. It worked. Best job ever.'

Hook nodded. Angels all over the world instead of armies. It had been a bright new dawn and, like Jared said, it had worked. Everyone getting along and letting the angels protect and serve. And the Games to entertain. He and Jared had been at the forefront of the new world order and they had made it work.

Stella leant against the outside of the Natural History Museum. The trees were huge but she could still see that the deads on the roads were more numerous now, a dozen or so scattered across the once-busy tarmac. She imagined the cars thronging the roads, the trees neatly pruned, the people on the pavements, the cyclists, the buses. The noise. So much noise and now nothing. A city of millions just a dusty, overgrown tomb populated with the dead.

They could never clear them all, she realised. There would never be enough batteries or thumpers to let them move through the city. Or they would reach their limit and they would have nothing but the garden. Stella knew it would never be enough and that one day she would be too slow and a dead or an angel would kill her.

She reached down to the tanto strapped at her thigh and pulled it out of its sheath in one smooth motion. The long blade glinted in the sunlight as she raised it high. It was in the dead's head as soon as it poked itself out of the window, its body slung across the high window sill. Stella dragged it forward so that its waist was on the sill. The next dead followed insensibly after and soon joined its fellow. She piled the bodies high, blocking the smashed window.

Patting the topmost dead on the back, she said, 'Thank you,' and trotted across to the window at the bottom of the left hand tower. Fishing in the pockets of her combat pants, she pulled out a pair of glass suckers and a glass cutter. She quickly scored a rectangle big enough for her to squeeze through and lifted the pane away with the suckers.

Inside were two more deads. 'Shhh,' she said to them, placing her finger to her lips.

They were on her as soon as she entered. The tanto was out of its sheath and up into the first dead's head in an instant. The second she allowed to come close before finishing it off with the same quiet efficiency.

She crept to the open door and peered into the main building. The huge arched chamber, the skeleton of the diving blue whale and the deads. The latter were crowded around the door to the chamber at the bottom of the other tower.

Smiling to herself, she crept to the staircase and began the climb to the top.

Stella the Zombie Killer Part Eight

Stella glided up the stairs, her big boots seeming to barely touch the steps. Deads were dealt with carefully but swiftly, each one receiving the tanto's blade up through its chin and into its brain before it could fully react to her presence. She caught each one, laying it gently on to the steps so as to create no sound, no fuss.

At the top of the tower there was nothing, not simply an absence of a mobile phone mast but nothing, just an empty, sun-striped space, with a single corpse, one arm outstretched, the other bent and stiff, the fingers on the hand pointing at her. Rats sat atop the hand and across the arm. They froze, whipping just their heads around to face her.

Ignoring the rats, she stared out of the narrow, arched windows onto a silent city. The other tower stood opposite. 'Good job somebody didn't just put a couple of dozen deads at the bottom of that tower,' she said to herself. 'Oh wait...'

Sighing, she moved back down the stairs, making no effort to cover her footsteps.

At the bottom, she saw the crowd of deads had already started to drift from the room's doorway. 'Come on then, guys, let's go again.' She ran at the skeleton of the blue whale suspended from the ceiling and jumped at its mouth, grabbing the jaw bone and swinging herself to a sitting position. Taking the tanto from its sheath, she ran the blade along the bones, tap, tap, tap.

The deads' heads jerked around at the noise and they began their broken journey towards Stella. Already deads were filing out of the room at the bottom of the other tower and making their way towards her.

'You guys are so cool,' she said. 'Look at the way you move. You'd have cleaned up at the break dance competitions.' Shifting herself on the whale's jaw, she reached back and gripped a bone. 'You need this?' she said to the whale. 'Didn't think so.' She yanked the bone from its socket and pulled it free from the wiring that held it in place. The entire

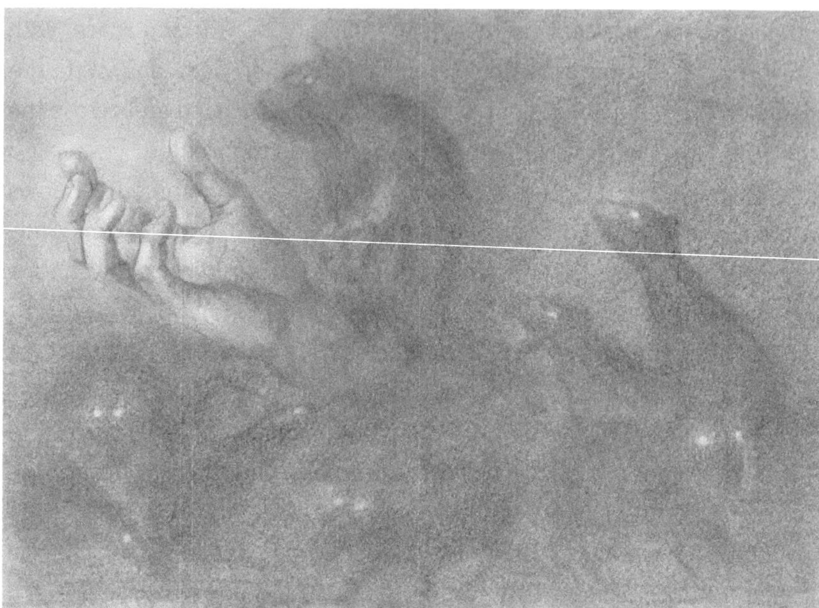

structure wobbled. 'Woah, Blue. Calm down. I'm not Jonah and I don't need spitting out.'

The deads looked up at her, shuffling to stand beneath.

The whale's skeleton shook again.

'Really?' said Stella. 'One bone and the whole lot comes down?'

There was a snap and a jerk. Stella slipped one way, her weight forcing the whale over and snapping more wires. 'There really wasn't much consideration for health and safety in getting you up here, Blue.' She shifted her body, getting her feet firmly on the jaw bone of the creature and snapping more wires. 'Still,' she said, 'you've gotta work with what you've got.' She swung down at the deads, their filthy, clawed hands reached out to her desperately, like bloodied front row fans at a rock concert.

Stella brought the bone round in a vicious arc, clubbing the front three out of the way. Their skulls smashed obligingly and Stella leapt back down to the floor, leaving the skeleton swinging wildly. 'This way!' she shouted and hurried beneath the swaying bones. She held her own bone up and rattled it along the whale's ribcage. She could see that more and more deads were filing out of the room at the bottom of the tower. 'C'mon, guys, this is where the meat's at. Come and get it!' She battered the skeleton with her length of bone, beating a rhythm that hypnotised the deads, pulling them beneath the whale.

The skeleton dropped several inches as more wires snapped.

Stella leapt in the air, grabbed the rib cage with one hand and began to swing the construct back and forth, batting any deads that came within reach with her bone. Stella grunted with the effort as she swung on the skeleton and batted away two more deads. As she felt more wires snapping, she gave a great heave and swung the whale away and back at the deads. She clicked her heels together to bring blades from the front of both of her boots and kicked a couple out of the way, stabbing into their brains as she did it, before swinging back again. On this pass, she felt more wires giving way. She allowed the skeleton to reach its peak and then threw her bone down to grip the rib cage as hard as she could before pushing the whale with all her strength back towards the deads and then dropping to the ground.

As she rolled to her feet, the final wires snapped, sending the skeleton crashing into the deads gathered beneath. The clattering noise was deafening as bones pummelled the museum floor and the stumbling monsters, battering them to the ground and tangling them in a skeletal avalanche.

Quickly circling the area, the quiet sound of her knife replacing the clatter of the bones, Stella took out deads with the speed and efficiency that earned her the nickname 'Killer' in the Games.

'Did you hear that?' said Jared.

'Could hardly miss it,' said Hook. He dropped his spade and moved towards the building. 'Fancy a trip out, Captain?' he said over his shoulder.

Jared stared. He saw his old camp. Three summers and three winters, barely surviving, watching people dying, killing the bitten, burning the bodies and hiding from the angels. The summers stinking and hot, the smell of rotten flesh permanently in his nostrils, death the only constant. The winters so empty, so stark, the cold like a million deads swarming his body, biting at exposed flesh, pulling at his clothes, stretching them thinner. The hunger gnawing at his insides, the constant ache for food, for comfort threatening to overwhelm him, to consume him, his own body ready to mutiny and devour him whole. The desperate trek back to the city with the few who could make it. The angels. The people's need. The failure.

'No worries,' said Hook. Concern filled his eyes as he looked to Jared. 'You keep resting and recovering. Although if you could tie off those runner beans, that'd be great.' The big man smiled and walked away.

In a daze, Jared moved to the runner beans and began tying them to the canes Hook had already put in place.

The images had flashed through his mind in just a few seconds. Now they were indelibly etched into his vision. He couldn't look at anything without seeing his people sliced by the angels' lasers, or the face of a dead lurching into their camp, seeing it bite deeply into a girl's shoulder. As if the flashes of memory were not enough, as if he hadn't suffered enough, his brain showed him details; the girl was thirteen, her parents dead, the ward of the camp, protected and loved by all. Jared had watched her die and then driven an axe into her skull. Her name was Julie. And Jared had killed her.

'No,' he said aloud. 'It was the deads. We couldn't stop them all.'

But he couldn't persuade himself; his vision filled with Julie's face, twisted in agony as she was bitten. Her face as she died. No peace. Just pain. Her skull cleaved. His hand on the haft.

He flinched, not noticing that he pulled the beans away from the canes.

He screwed his eyes shut, squeezing them as tightly as he could, burying his fists into the eye sockets until he could feel the pain and the pressure on his eyeballs.

He could crush them, he realised. He could force them through his head and into his brain.

He squeezed tighter.

He stumbled.

Someone caught him. Their strong arms wrapped around his thin frame and lowered him gently to the ground.

Stella ran to the room at the bottom of the other tower where she had earlier dealt with the three deads. She leapt over the corpse with the huge, old-fashioned monitor still crushing its skull, and made her way up the stairs. The cacophony she had raised with the whale meant that the deads were already coming down to meet her, but she had no trouble dispatching them; her blade was into their heads and their bodies were left to clatter on the steps in half-second attacks.

At the top of the tower there was a mast. Stella knew that it was what she was looking for, covered as it was with antenna and satellite dishes. It stretched from floor to ceiling, and Stella could see that the very top would poke up and out of the roof.

She produced a yellow multi-meter from her pocket and pulled the red and yellow prongs free of the unit. Gregor had already set the device up to measure voltage and told her where to place the prongs and then all she had to do was make a note of the number. The prongs in place, she switched the multi meter on.

Nothing.

She tapped it against her leg.

Nothing. Zero. An actual zero on the small screen. The mast was not operational.

Hook stalked the street outside the Victoria and Alert, smashing any zombies' heads that came close enough. A couple of dozen had been attracted by the noise but they were spread out. His weapon of choice was a mace; a metre-long shaft of wood and metal topped with a metal orb covered in vicious spikes. It dripped blood and gore and Hook held it firmly in his hands, like a bat.

The Natural History Museum loomed behind him as he cleared enough space to allow himself to turn his back on the zombies and head over to the imposing building.

The zombies' bodies laid over the sill of the smashed window of the tower on the right drew his attention. He looked over the corpses into the room. Empty.

A noise behind him. Jet packs. Angels.

Hook leapt over the bodies and into the room.

Stella the Zombie Killer Part Nine

'Easy,' said Gregor. 'I think you had quite a nasty turn.' He was helping Jared into a chair at what was the Victoria and Albert reception desk and was now Gregor's workshop and general meeting place for the team.

Jared liked teams. The army was all about team building. He was happy in a team. Gregor, Hook and Stella. What about Jared?

'I'll not tell Hook that you knocked his runner beans over. He'll be upset about that. We'll say the wind got them,' said Gregor.

'Yeah,' said Jared. His voice was distant, like it came from his mouth and fell to the floor before he could hear it properly. He glanced down, half expecting to see his voice as some sort of sick child staring back up at him.

'You gonna be sick?' asked Gregor.

Jared shook his head and winced as the effort produced dots swimming before his eyes and sent his brain spinning. Gregor's hands were on his shoulders again, steadying him.

'You've been out there from the beginning.' It wasn't a question.

Jared, unable to speak, nodded just once. A tear caught in the corner of his eye, balled and fell onto his cheek. He made no effort to arrest its slide down his face.

Gregor watched it, nodded grimly. 'You need more rest. More food and then more rest. We'll eat.' He busied himself in his work space, shifting huge pieces of angel armour and equipment out of his way. 'Your little run-in with the angels is going to prove very useful. Hook and Stella both have lots of parts in need of repair; a lot of this stuff will end up in them or on them.'

Jared looked around the sharp, metallic piles. 'Will you turn them into angels?'

The tech laughed. 'No, I don't think so. Reckon neither of them wants to share their heads with a machine.' He tapped his temple as he spoke. 'No, this stuff will be used to fix them. I was a Games coach,' Gregor added by way of explanation.

Jared nodded. Games coaches were basically bio-engineers in charge of the teams' augmentations. The Cynosure Games had been so popular because they were so different from anything that had come before. Each contestant, team or individual games, was physically augmented. All of them were stronger, faster, quicker. 'Were you with Stella in the Games?' he asked.

Gregor nodded. 'We worked together for five years, scoring points, winning games. She was the 'Killer' and I was the 'Fixer'. Rest of the team used to change pretty regularly, injuries, retirements and so on, but Stella, she was there from beginning to end.'

None of this was new to Jared. An all-rounder, Stella had competed in the individual and team games. She was the Killer, the Cynosure, had been for three years in a row, and was the most exciting talent the two years before that. She was the most famous person in the world. A whole planet at her feet. 'The Cynosure fights for you,' whispered Jared.

'And she still does, in her way,' said Gregor. 'No more games but still plenty to do, plenty of points to score, people to fight for.' He nodded at Jared to remind him who had insisted that he come into their place. He bent to rummage for a tin in a cupboard. 'We normally try and vary the food a bit but I think you need something quick and easy.' He opened the tin of beans and sausages, poured them in a bowl and placed it in the microwave. 'I heard Hook call you Captain. You were army?'

Jared nodded, listening with renewed wonder to the purr of the microwave.

'When did you get out?' Gregor asked.

'Stayed till the end. Once the Message arrived and the governments came on board, we knew that the army's time was up. But there was plenty to do to get everything decommissioned. I was very busy.'

'Was it easy to leave?'

'No,' said Jared. 'No, I'd been career military. The army was as much family as my family.' The fatigue was making him speak more freely than he usually would and so he was grateful for the excuse to stop talking when Gregor placed the bowl of steaming food in front of him.

'And after?' said Gregor.

'Angel control.'

Gregor nodded as if it were obvious. 'You know about these things?' he indicated the angels' parts on the benches.

Jared shook his head. 'Logistics and strategies,' he said. 'Nothing on maintenance or design.'

'Shame. Would've been useful.'

Stella jogged down the stairs, jumping over the bodies of the deads. Her blade was strapped to her thigh, her short sweat-plastered hair close to her head, sweat gleamed on her bare arms and her face shined with energy.

'You enjoying yourself?' said Hook as he moved up the steps to meet her. The mace was held casually at his side.

They both stopped. Stella smiled. 'Nope.' She watched the blood and gore drip from the spikes on his mace.

'The mess downstairs says otherwise,' said Hook.

Stella smiled again. 'Nothing here. No charge on the phone mast. We should go. I can check out another building before dark.'

Hook shook his head. 'Too late. I heard jet packs.'

Stella sighed with annoyance. 'Since when does noise bring them?'

'Since their scanners stopped working, maybe?' said Hook, shrugging his massive shoulders.

Stella caught sight of the titanium beneath his t-shirt. 'Make an effort,' she said, nodding to his chest.

'Who's gonna see? Or care?' He looked her up and down meaningfully. 'We can't all have perfect augments. You know I was one of the earlier ones. Skin doesn't always fit, especially on hot days.'

Stella wrinkled her face in disgust. 'You could still make an effort with it.'

Hook looked like he was about to argue, but he stopped, moving down a couple of steps till he was level with Stella. 'Listen, Stella,' he began.

But Stella cut him off. 'Later,' she said. 'If there are angels about, we'd best head home; can't be lucky two days in a row.'

Hook nodded but didn't move. He barred her way.

Stella held her arms out, questioning the bigger man.

Eventually Hook moved to one side and held his arm out to allow her to pass, pointing the way down the steps with his mace. 'Lead the way, boss.'

Stella, glaring at him all the way, moved past him and down the steps.

'Are you sure?' said Jared. 'I want to pull my weight.'

'Well' said Gregor, looking him up and down and taking in the skinny figure, 'that's not very much, so you've done your bit for today.'

Jared nodded gratefully. 'Shall I sleep in Stella's room again?'

'Best not. We need to get you a place of your own.' Gregor guided him past the curtained gift shop. 'So, Captain, eh?'

Jared nodded.

'When did you first hear about the disbandment?'

'Soldiers were the last to know for sure. You guys probably knew better than us from watching the TV.' Jared paused to catch his breath. He was so much more tired than he realised. 'Still came as a shock though. No more army. No more armies!'

'It was a hell of a message,' said Gregor.

Jared nodded. 'An offer too good to refuse.'

'Any idea what happened? See anything in angel control?'

'The same as everyone else. Four ships, four missiles. Four crashes. One apocalypse.'

Gregor nodded. They moved into the cafeteria and Gregor guided Jared to benches along the wall. Hook's garden could be seen from the window. He helped Jared lower himself to the bench.

'I'm sorry to be so useless,' said Jared.

Gregor shook his head. 'You've survived for three years since the crash. I reckon we can make you useful.'

Stella and Hook were still on the stairs when the sound of smashing glass stopped them.

Turning carefully, Stella looked back and up at Hook, her finger on her lips.

Hook nodded.

They both waited, listening intently.

All they could hear was the faint sound of the deads still struggling in the bones of the blue whale.

Then the heavy tread of metal boots on broken glass.

Stella pointed back up the stairs. *Go*, she mouthed.

The two of them moved up the stairs as quickly and quietly as they could. Stella wished that she was alone. Hook was good for taking care of deads and smashing windows but he wasn't quick enough for angels. As they made their painfully slow way back up to the top of the tower, she stared at his back, bitter that he had come for her.

Finally they made it to the open door at the top of the steps and the two of them made a dash for it.

Just as they reached the last step Hook stumbled, his booted foot catching on the edge of the step.

Stella reached out to him but it was no use. Once his bulky frame was falling there was no stopping him.

He crashed to the dusty floor, his mace flying free, scattering across the floor, the noise loud enough to wake the dead. Stella saw him turn his fall into a roll and tumble into the room. She dashed in, turned and closed the door as quietly as she could. She glared at big man.

He shrugged apologetically, mouthing *Sorry* at her.

Stella stalked towards him, her face grim. She stopped as she heard the noise: heavy solid footsteps. Not slow, not hurried. Purposeful. Stella pointed Hook towards the far corner and took up a position opposite. She made a gesture across her throat to Hook and then pointed at the door. She indicated herself and held up one finger before pointing back to Hook with two fingers raised.

Hook nodded his understanding. He glanced at his mace but Stella shook her head. Just be ready, the instruction.

They waited for long seconds, the footsteps louder with each tread.

The firm grip of a gauntleted hand on the handle. The handle turning slowly, irresistibly.

Stella was on the balls of her feet, ready as the door swung open. The first movement of bulky white armour, an arm, a leg, a chest plate, a helmeted face.

She launched at the angel, leaping high into the air, avoiding its grasping arms and wrapping her arms around the face of the helmet, using the creature's head to slingshot around to its back.

Hook roared, setting off a split second after her and slamming into the angel's torso. With Stella on its back and Hook at the front the cyborg tottered, stumbled and fell.

Stella skilfully moved herself out from under the falling angel and had her hands on its throat ready to squeeze and tear while Hook held it down.

The three of them came crashing down onto the steps, the angel's armour acting as a toboggan and sliding down the steep incline.

Stella had to readjust quickly, her hands flying from its throat to its shoulders and then jamming her knees into its armpits so as to hang on.

Hook flailed and tried to grab the angel's ankles, but missed, and Stella and the angel were gone, banging down the first flight of steps to crash on the landing below.

As the angel hit the landing, Stella was up, pushing her feet into its chest to slam its helmeted head into the wall. Immediately, she was ready to attack him again, not waiting for Hook to lumber down the steps to help. She whipped her tanto blade from her thigh and bent to the creature's chin.

'Wait!' The voice didn't come from Hook.

Stella stopped mid-strike.

'I'm alive!' It was coming from the angel. It was raising its hands and pushing at its helmet. 'I'm alive!' it repeated.

Stella stood back, her tanto still raised, just as Hook joined her.

'What the...?' he said as the angel raised its helmet.

It was a man. Two-thirds of his face was flesh. Around his right eye and across his cheekbone to his ear was metal. Shining silver metal.

'My name is Vine,' he said, 'Michael Vine.' He was breathing hard. He looked up at Stella and Hook, his left eye strong, his pale blue right eye unblinking. 'And I'm alive.'

Stella the Zombie Killer Part Ten

The street in front of the Natural History Museum was silent. Deads drifted towards the broken windows at the bottom of the towers, drawn by the noise and the arrival of the angel. They were slow and awkward, disinterested; their movements fluid, inevitable, heavy, like tar sliding down a window on a hot day. Soon there was a cluster of them around the base of the towers, spilling to stand stubbornly in front of the heavy doors.

Gregor watched from the high windows of the Victoria and Albert, his eyes darting backwards and forwards over the growing crowd. He nodded grimly and made his decision.

'Alive?' said Hook. 'How is he alive? I've not seen a live angel since the crash.'

'Me neither,' said Stella, 'but look at him. He's alive.'

Michael Vine, the living angel, sat in the corner of the room at the top of one of the Natural History Museum's towers. Sort of in the corner; the space wasn't big enough for him, and so the bulk of his white armour meant that he sat somewhere closer to the middle of the room. Through the doorway, he regarded Stella and Hook coolly, as if he found it slightly amusing that they might consider themselves his captors.

Stella and Hook looked over their shoulders at the man/machine. They were standing on the landing outside of the room. He stared back, completely unfazed. 'I think he's okay,' Stella whispered.

'You think everyone's okay,' Hook replied. He pulled Stella away from the doorway and whispered urgently. 'What are you gonna do, check his wrists and ankles and invite him home for tea?'

Stella looked up at Hook's face, saw the deep mistrust and the bitterness and the regret. 'He's a man, a person. We save people.'

'You're not the Cynosure, not anymore. You can't save everybody, Stella.'

'I can save the ones I find.'

'Change the record. We can't take it. We can't trust it. We can't feed it.'

'*He* is a person. *He* will be trustworthy. *He* will need to pull his weight, which in *his* case is a bit more than the rest of us. *He* can find the extra food.'

Hook stepped back from her, his hands moving to his shaggy hair and pulling at it. 'This is too much. He's an angel. Angels are bad. Remember those hot lasers? How many times have we had to hide from them?'

'Actually,' said Vine. He raised his voice to be heard through the doorway. 'I can't shoot you. My laser's deactivated.' His voice was deep, altered in some way, or affected by his cybernetics.

'Nice going, meathead,' said Stella. She turned away from him and walked into the room. 'Mr Vine, I apologise for my partner's comments. He doesn't always see an opportunity, even when it's painted with ten foot letters on the side of a merry-go-round.' She glanced sideways at Hook as he entered the room.

Vine's presence made Hook seem less large than usual. He walked in with less certainty than was his habit.

Stella glanced at him, a slight smirk on her face.

'Just Vine is fine,' said the angel. 'And you're the Killer.'

'Not for a long time. At least not in the ring.'

Vine nodded. 'And you're Hook. Centre back for the Falcons,' he said.

Hook couldn't help but smile.

'You never played together,' Vine continued. 'You could have made it with the Mariners.' He pointed at Hook as he said this. Hook again failed to hide his smile.

'You liked the Games?' said Hook.

Vine shrugged. 'My kid. At least at first. He saw a year of the Games.'

'There were five,' said Stella. 'Did he get bored? Because they got better once we adapted the augments.'

'I know,' said Vine. 'I carried on watching after he died. It reminded me of him.'

'Oh,' said Stella. 'I'm sorry.'

Hook moved between them. 'You said something about your laser not working.'

'Inhibitors,' said Vine. 'They're in place to stop me firing on humans. Only someone in Angel Control can release it. And then only a commander. I'm no threat to you.'

'So you say,' said Hook.

'I've followed you for the last week...'

Stella cut him off. 'No chance. We'd have known. You can't get close to us without our hearing you.'

'I don't need to be close.' He tapped the top of his metal cheekbone, right below his blue robotic eye.

'Way to earn our trust, Officer Murphy,' said Hook.

'A Robocop reference.' Vine smiled. 'I haven't heard one of those since my wife was alive.'

'Angels could be married?' said Stella.

'Of course,' said Vine. 'But I was divorced.'

The three of them stood awkwardly for a moment. Stella marvelled at the situation; three altered humans surrounded by the undead, not knowing what to say to someone who had declared that his child was dead and that he had lost his wife twice.

'Sounds like you crashed well before the ships did,' she said.

Vine nodded.

'Is that why you volunteered for the angels?' said Hook.

Vine nodded again. 'Pretty much.'

Gregor grabbed a thumper from the table and headed for the front doors. Lifting the bar, he paused. He remembered Jared lying on the bench in the cafeteria. He shrugged, trusting that the captain would sleep through it. He looked at the door. He wouldn't be able to lock it. They hadn't left the museum empty for years. Gregor had not left for years.

He pulled the door open and slipped outside, closing the door as quietly as he could behind him. A zombie, shuffling towards the Natural History Museum, noticed him, while the rest remained unaware. Gregor had heard Hook and Stella talking about the zombies' reactions and how slow they were. He decided to risk leaving this one and moved quickly to find cover behind a tall lamppost. He had the thumper inside a shoulder bag and carried a heavy sword taken from one of the exhibits in both hands. The weight of it was causing him some regret and he considered going back to change it, but the more he moved, the more zombies would notice him. He pushed on, padding to a bench and ducking behind it. Another zombie had noticed him and one of the ones close to him jerked around, matching its partner's movements. It would follow the other even if it wasn't aware of Gregor.

He crouched and ran awkwardly to the red phone box and then on to the trees, so wildly overgrown that even a gentle breeze made them loud enough to cover his footsteps.

He hoped.

Looking around the trunk of a tree he thought he could count five zombies heading for him. For now, the majority were still shuffling towards the Natural History Museum but that could quickly change. Stella had told him of the erratic behaviour of the creatures and how you couldn't predict with certainty what they were going to do. As he watched, another two noticed the actions of their peers and turned to face him.

Gregor tried to control his breathing. His ears rang with sound, and he tried to quell the rising panic. This wasn't such a good idea. The short distance back to Vic's was already blocked by zombies. They were spread out and he could probably run between them as he had heard Stella describe, but he wasn't confident. The sword was too heavy for more than a few swings before he would tire. He wished he had Stella's speed or Hook's strength.

Looking across the road, he remembered that if he didn't get the thumper placed then no one would have Stella and Hook.

Precious moments had been wasted already. Taking a deep breath, he ran across the road.

Without realising it, his hiding place had created a blind spot and he ran straight into one of the creatures, knocking it and himself over. His knee connected with the knee of the zombie and he felt it bend and snap as his weight fell onto it. He rolled over, dropping the sword, sending it clattering along the road. More zombies turned their heads at the sound and the one on the ground was already reaching for him, its dead eyes staring and its jaws moving mechanically.

Gregor crawled backwards on his bottom, kicking away from it. When his hand touched the sword he remembered Hook and Stella's tales about never moving backwards. He stumbled to his feet and hefted the sword, walking slowly back to the zombie as it dragged itself towards him. Draggers are easier than shufflers, he told himself. Draggers are easier than shufflers. He raised the sword, ready to strike. Lowered it again. Raised it. Lowered it. He stared into the creature's face. As he did, he realised he had again been walking backwards to keep a distance between it and him. He threw a look over his shoulder. Three of them, almost within grabbing distance.

'Give me a break!' he hissed at them and ran for the other side of the road, past more trees and on into the overgrown green space of Egerton Gardens.

It was a huge horseshoe of tall town houses, all of them five stories, their faded paintwork dark against the brilliant blue sky. Each of them was empty; Stella and Hook had scouted and looted them in the first months after the crash, but, Gregor supposed, that didn't mean zombies hadn't moved in since.

'Stick to the plan,' he mumbled to himself. The houses were a fantastic bottleneck and he could escape through one of them and back to Vic's. That was the plan.

He was half a minute or so ahead of the zombies by the time he came to the house at the furthest point from the entrance to the horseshoe. Plenty of time to set up the thumper and make a run for it.

Pulling it from his bag, he flicked the on switch, took one rueful look at the twelve batteries attached to it, and placed it on the front door step.

He tried the handle of the front door. Locked. He ran next door, the first zombies already moving through the overgrown greenery in his direction. Desperately, he rattled at the handle. He took a moment to stare at the zombies; dozens of them already, slowly making their way towards him.

Stela stared at the angel. 'You fell,' she said.

Vine looked at her, his face thoughtful as he considered her words. 'I suppose I did.'

'Why us?' said Hook. 'You said you've been watching us. Why us?'

Vine shrugged, the tectonic movements of shoulder and breast plates strangely quiet. 'The Cynosure,' he said, pointing at and then turning to Stella. 'Once I saw you, I knew that I had to see if you were still...' he shrugged again. 'I don't know, decent, I suppose.'

'She's not a saint, you know,' said Hook.

'Or an angel,' said Stella.

'I know,' said Vine. He shrugged again. 'We should try to start again, and you're someone that can bring people together. Tash and I agreed on that.'

'Tash?' said Stella.

'Six months ago I rescued her. I was in Peterborough. She was trapped in a Sainsbury's. She'd been hiding there since the crash and the zombies finally got in. We've been on the road together ever since. Thought we'd find more people in London.'

'Where is she?' said Stella.

'Not far from here. I came to talk to you alone, make sure it was okay for us both to come to you.'

'We're not Butlin's,' said Hook.

'It's not an argument,' said Stella. 'They both come, simple as that.'

Hook stared at her, but he remained silent.

'This Tash survived on her own for more than two years?' Stella asked.

Vine nodded.

'Then she'll be useful,' said Stella, looking pointedly at Hook.

'And she can cut hair,' said Vine, pointing at Hook's unruly mop.

Hook smiled back sarcastically.

Vine stood.

Hook stayed still.

Stella stepped between them. 'We can compare muscles later,' she said. She glared at them both as neither man stepped away. 'We're not doing this.'

Vine turned away.

Hook smiled at the back of head and got a jab in the ribs from Stella.

'Let's go,' she said.

'Might be easier said than done,' said Vine. He was staring out of the window, down at the street.

Hook joined him. 'There's a party down there,' he said. 'And even the Cynosure didn't get an invite.' He glanced at Stella who was deliberately ignoring him. 'Of course,' he continued, 'if someone hadn't sent an entire blue whale crashing to the floor, this wouldn't be a problem.'

'Whatever,' Stella said to Hook.

'It was very loud,' Vine added.

'Whatever,' she said to Vine. She turned to the window and looked down at the crowd. 'All the other exits are barricaded.' She pursed her lips thoughtfully. 'We push our way out,' she said.

'What about our laser-less friend?' Hook asked.

Stella thought she could hear an amused tone in his voice, but she glanced at Vine and raised her eyebrows

'Just because I can't fire a laser at them doesn't mean I can't hit them,' Vine replied. He clenched his massive metal-gloved fists for emphasis. Hook pretended not to notice. Stella sighed.

'Wait,' she said. 'They're leaving.'

The three of them stared down from their high vantage point. The deads were definitely beginning to drift away.

'Did they just get fed up?' said Hook

'No,' said Vine. 'They're all heading in the same direction.' He pointed across the road and to the left. 'Something is attracting them.'

'Thumper,' said Stella. 'Gregor.' She shook her head. 'Stupid.'

'Where's he gone with it?' Hook asked, scanning the area.

'What's a thumper?' said Vine.

'It sends out ultra sound waves,' said Stella. 'They attract the deads.'

'Ultra sound?' said Vine. 'I can track that and maybe find your friend.'

'Wow,' said Hook sarcastically. 'You're like a magic box, just full of tricks and surprises! Can you make toast as well?'

Stella ignored him. 'Yes, please, Mr Vine. Gregor hasn't been outside for two years; he's not ready. Chances are he's blundered about and got dozens of them following him. The thumper'll only work if the deads can't see anyone. They'll go for him over an ultra sound any time.'

'Call me Vine.' The cyborg's electric blue eye flickered. 'Scanning now,' he said.

Stella smiled at Hook. 'He's gonna be useful.'

Hook shrugged.

'Across the road,' said Vine. He pointed in the same direction as before.

'I think we knew that much,' said Hook.

'I can follow the signal to its precise location, but would your friend still be there? It doesn't seem sensible to set off this thumper and then stand next to it. I assume he knows what it does.'

Hook nodded begrudgingly.

'The thumper is in a place called Egerton Gardens,' Vine added. He saw the quizzical looks on the other two's faces. He lifted his hand to the metal side of his head and tapped it with his fore finger. The metallic chink of sound echoed slightly. 'I have maps,' he said.

Stella nodded. 'The big posh houses. They're not far. We cleaned them out last year.' Hook nodded his agreement. 'They're set out in a ring with one entrance. If he's in there he's trapped.'

'He could hide in the houses,' Vine pointed out.

Stella shook her head. 'Hook and me made sure all the doors were locked so that the houses couldn't get any surprise guests.' She paused, thinking hard. 'Gregor would have to smash a window. We get over there, look for that and we'll know where he is. Otherwise...' She left the otherwise unspoken.

'I can go now,' said Vine.

Stella looked at the angel, realised what he was suggesting. She nodded her head.

The three of them clattered down the steps and out into the main entrance hall of the museum. Hook had retrieved his mace and Stella still had her tanto strapped to her thigh. Vine went to the fallen skeleton, smashing a dead in the face as he went. Even Hook nodded his approval as the dead's head seem to fold in on itself. Other deads, sprawled among the bones, tried to reach him, but just pawed ineffectually against his leg armour.

Vine grabbed a huge bone, at least two-and-a-half-metres long and sharp at one end and thick at the other. He twirled it around in front of him, the noise it made swirling through the air was audible to Stella and Hook. He turned and quickly stabbed the heads of each of the deads still trapped in the bones and then stalked back towards Stella and Hook. 'Let's go,' he said.

Gregor stood atop the front steps of a house three doors down from the thumper. The zombies ignored the device, preferring the promise of fresh meat. He looked over the railing to the basement; if that was locked as well, then he would be trapped.

Some of the undead had reached the path and in seconds his escape would be blocked. He hefted the sword in both of his hands. Go now and he'd only have to kill one to get to the next door. He could work his way from door to door, killing one zombie at a time.

But he was scared.

He stood rooted to the spot, waiting for the first one to come to him. Over their heads he could see more of them entering the mews. The central grassy area was dotted with trees. He tried to guess the distance. Ten metres. Twenty metres. Fewer than ten zombies between him and the tree. A dash of a few seconds, nothing more. The next tree was a similar distance, a similar dash, a similar number of zombies.

He stepped down, ready to go, the sword gripped tightly in both hands.

It was too much. He stepped back. The closest zombie took another step forward. Drool spilled from its mouth as it gnashed its teeth, its arms lifting, its hands reaching.

Gregor held the sword out at it, batting at its hands. It grabbed at the blade uselessly, like a robot with a dysfunctional programme.

'Get back!' he shouted at it. He stabbed at its hands, drawing blood.

The creature came on.

The weight of the sword was suddenly enormous in Gregor's hands. The point wavered in front of him, his arms unable to support the sword, the blade dropping. He willed it to stay in the air but it drooped in front of his eyes, out of his control, like a bridge lowering into an unseen river.

The zombie lurched forward, catching its foot on the top step and falling into Gregor. It looked up at him, blood erupting from its mouth, the blade of the sword, deep in its stomach, keeping it at bay.

Gregor held on but the weight was too much; he dropped with the zombie falling onto him, pushing him down, leaning its head forward and snapping its teeth.

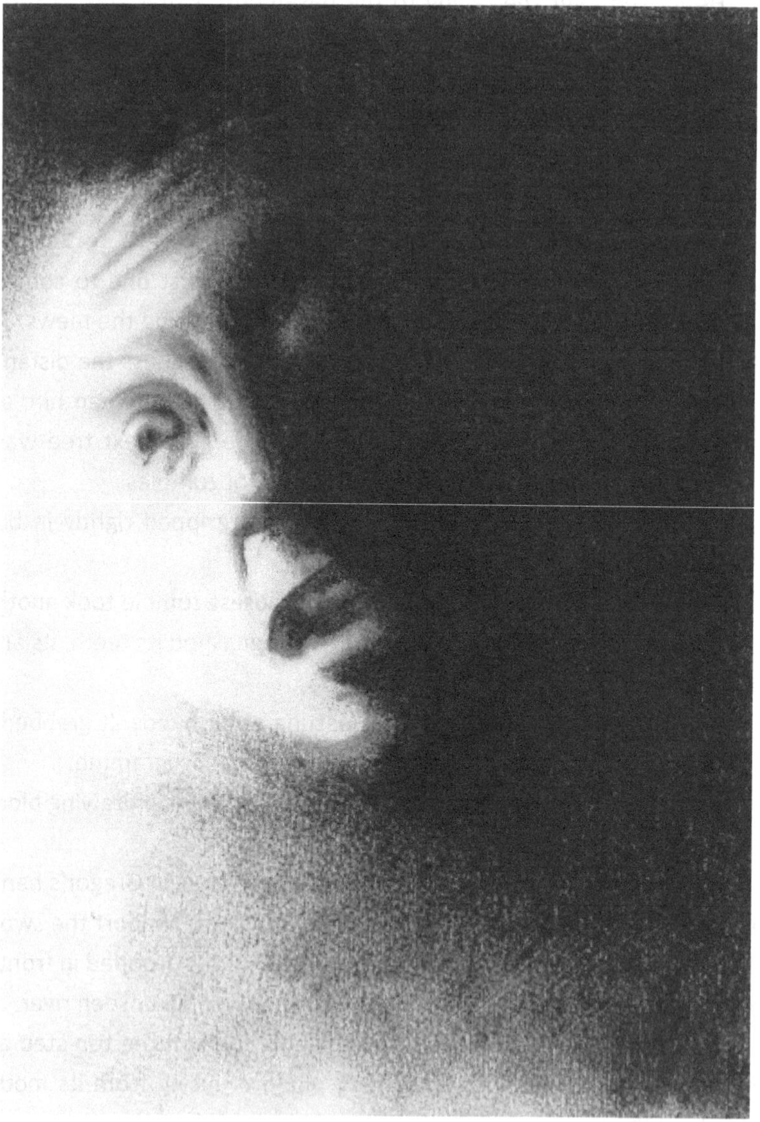

With his elbows braced against the hard concrete of the step he was able to hold the zombie a few inches from his face. He could feel the blood pouring down the handle of the sword, the red liquid mixing with the sweat on his hands. The handle slipped, the pommel pushed against his chest, the zombie's face another inch closer.

Something grabbed his ankle. He kicked out in fright, dislodging the grip but the clawed hands were reaching for him again.

And then the sound of a jet pack.

Gregor groaned. He kicked with legs and turned his face as far from the zombie as possible, bloody drool dripping and sliding on top his cheek.

It was over. He knew that now. He stopped kicking and let go of the sword, the pommel sinking into his chest, making him exhale in pain as the zombie's face fell onto him, its forehead butting his nose, causing blood to flow. Hands grabbed his ankle and began to pull at him. The zombie on his chest lifted its head and Gregor felt the creature's teeth graze against his face, its mouth begin to close.

Suddenly, it was yanked away from him and he could see the sky, so blue, so clear. The hands were no longer reaching for his legs and the only sound was that of tearing and thumping. He lifted his head and his vision was filled with sight of an angel holding a huge bone in two huge hands. With every swing zombies were batted to the side, sent sprawling as they groped for the armoured figure.

It turned its head to him. 'You're Gregor, yes?'

Gregor nodded, wiping the blood and drool from his face.

'I'm Vine. Stella sent me.'

Gregor fell back against the hard concrete, the pain in his chest and nose competing with the flooding feeling of relief. He was alive.

Stella the Zombie Killer Part Eleven

'What were you thinking?' said Stella to a very pale Gregor. The four of them, Stella, Gregor, Hook and Vine, stood in the rotunda of the Victoria and Albert Museum. Three of them waited for Gregor's answer.

The bio-mech shook his head. 'Thought I could help. Thought I should help.'

Hook and Stella stared at him. 'Not your job, mate,' said Hook. 'You pull your weight. No worries on that score. You don't need to be running about taking on deads.'

'You don't need to be running about,' Stella added not unkindly. 'Look at the state of you. Heart attack'll get you before the deads.' She laughed gently, trying to ease Gregor from his panic.

Vine lumbered forwards. 'You should listen to your friends. Your heart rate is elevated, you are sweating and trembling, you are not listening properly, which means your ears are probably ringing, your breathing is shallow, your mouth is dry and, if it isn't already, your throat will soon be sore.'

Gregor stared at the angel, his eyes wide with terror.

Stella sighed at Vine. 'Thanks, machine man.' She turned again to Gregor. 'Just try to relax. It'll be okay.'

Vine interrupted Stella again. 'Your body is flooded with adrenaline. It would be best if you walked around.'

Stella and Hook stared at Vine. Hook shrugged. 'Makes sense,' he said, begrudgingly.

The two of them helped Gregor to his feet and walked him around the large ringed desk. Gregor's breathing echoed into the high roof but it was gradually slowing. They walked for five minutes, Stella and Hook staying with the tech, assuring him, placing comforting hands on his shoulders.

Vine watched them for a while and then turned his attention to the angel parts stacked on Gregor's work benches.

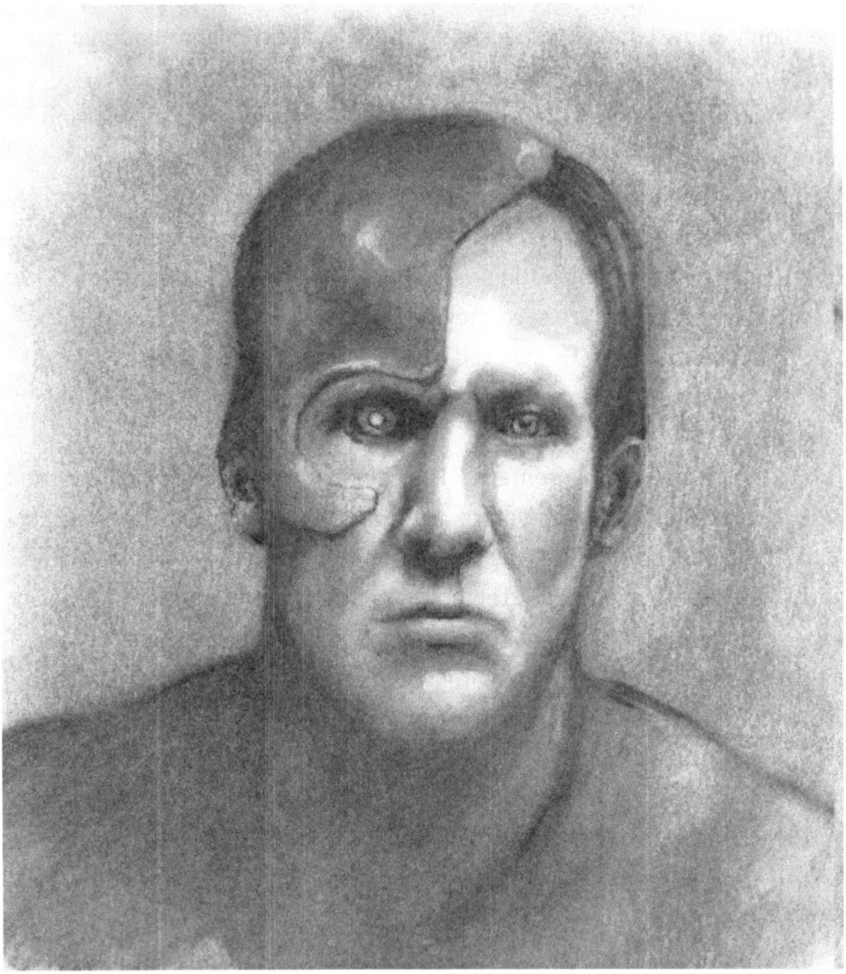

Stella watched the angel, carefully.

Gregor pushed her gently away. 'I'm okay,' he said. 'Go check on your new friend. Make sure he isn't stealing anything.'

Moving inside the circular desk, Stella approached Vine slowly as if she didn't know what to expect. As if his right arm might suddenly rise and point and shoot a hot red laser.

'You don't need to worry,' said Vine. 'I wouldn't harm you and I can't harm you.'

'I like that you said wouldn't first,' Stella replied.

Vine nodded. 'Trust is difficult. It always was but now even more so. You're taking a big risk by letting me in here.'

Stella shrugged. 'We save the ones we can.'

He looked over at Gregor and Hook. 'Not everyone agrees.'

'We save the ones we can,' Stella repeated. 'What's the point otherwise?'

Vine nodded in agreement. 'They follow you,' he said pointing at Hook and Gregor, 'because you're right and they don't want to have to make difficult decisions. You say you're not the boss...'

'You really have been listening,' said Stella, cutting him off. 'That is very creepy, you know? And where were you when we were fighting those angels? Could've done with some help there. *That* would've a pretty good way to earn a bit of trust.'

Vine shrugged. 'You're too fast. And I didn't think you would charge them. They were no threat to you, so you could have stayed out of sight.'

'Apparently not from you though.'

'I couldn't think of another way to assess whether or not you were safe for Tash and me.'

'When do we get to meet her?'

'I'll get her this afternoon.'

Stella nodded. 'I'll come with you. See where you've been hiding. And I need to pick up the dead angel we left yesterday. Don't suppose you've got any batteries?'

'No,' said Vine. 'I'm afraid not. You use them to power your 'thumpers'?'

Stella nodded. 'We're running low and Gregor's wasted another one today.'

The tech glanced over. 'Sorry,' he said. 'I am really sorry.'

'It's fine.' Stella waved away his apology. 'Heart in the right place and all that. But next time, don't, okay? Just don't.'

Gregor nodded and came back into the circle. He stepped carefully around Vine, staring up at the giant's stony face.

'You don't need to worry,' said Vine.

'I'm not worried,' said Gregor, trying to sound casual.

Vince leaned a little closer. 'You look worried.'

'Nope.' Gregor shook his head.

'I wouldn't want you to have another attack. You are safe around me. I wouldn't harm you and I couldn't harm you anyway.'

Gregor nodded. 'Good to know. Don't worry about me; I'm fine.'

'You're sure?'

'Yep.'

Stella laughed out loud. 'He's teasing you, Gregor,' she said. 'Don't let him blow your cover as a miserable old man. People will start to think you're human.'

Gregor grumbled his reply and set himself to work at the benches.

'You don't have to do that now,' said Stella. 'Take some time.'

'Yeah,' said Hook, hefting the sword that Gregor had taken outside with him. 'You need a rest after using this thing. It weighs more than my grandma! What made you choose this?'

Gregor shrugged. 'I thought it looked like it would hit hard.'

'Only if you can swing it hard,' said Hook.

Vine laughed, a deep rumble of a chuckle.

'Woah, toasters can laugh,' said Hook. 'Well, frak me.'

'Robocop to Battlestar Galactica?' said Vine. 'You do jump around the references.'

'I could jump around on a lot more than references,' said Hook. Stella heard the poorly veiled threat in his voice.

'Threatening me is pointless,' said Vine. 'I cannot hurt you.'

Hook shrugged. His face was a mask of suspicion, his eyes never leaving Vine's face as the angel returned the stare, his own face impassive.

'Where's Jared?' said Stella, trying to break the staring contest. She turned to Vine and started to explain how they had found Jared but the angel cut her off.

'Mr Jenks,' he said. 'You brought him yesterday.'

'Still creepy,' said Stella. 'Did you listen to us in here as well?'

'No,' said Vine. 'That would have seemed wrong.'

Hook snorted. 'A toaster with manners. Now there's a novelty.'

Stella turned on Hook. "'Manners burned in the crash,' remember?' she said, quoting Hook's own words back at him. 'It'll be nice to have someone around who doesn't do as they like whenever they like.'

'What's that supposed to mean?' Hook challenged, his voice rising.

'That you don't stick to what we agree.' Stella raised her voice to match Hook's. 'I didn't need you coming to the museum like some knight in shining armour. I had it under control.'

'You were making enough noise to wake the dead!'

Stella threw her hands in the air. 'Bit late for that!'

'You two!' said Gregor. 'Quiet down.'

'Gregor is right. It isn't sensible to make so much noise,' Vine added.

Hook ignored them both. 'It was a sloppy play. You put yourself and the rest of us in danger!'

'It's not a game, Hook. Get your head in the real world and out of the ring.'

'It's not me that's not taking this seriously. You're upset with me for coming to help? That's insane!'

'I didn't need your help. I was fine!'

'Yeah, you looked it, standing on the stairs with deads everywhere and an angel on the way.'

'It turned out okay, didn't it? And all you did was...'

'Turned out okay? Gregor could've died!' Hook shouted over Stella. 'He would've died if it wasn't for Metal Mickey. You're relying on luck!'

'No. I'm relying on me!' Stella thumped her chest as she said it.

'Is that what you think?'

'Yes!' Stella snapped the word at Hook, using it to whip him.

'Don't be ridiculous,' Hook replied, trying to deflect the word, but the hurt was obvious. 'Why take in every stray we find if that's what you think?'

'We'll be stronger as a group.'

'You're not making sense. You're on your own but you want to be part of a group. What is it, Stella, do you just need to save us and then keep us in here like exhibits? Are we trophies? It's not me that needs to get out of the ring, it's you. You're not the Cynosure anymore!'

Stella stared at Hook and laughed. 'You just slow me down. I'd have been out of that building and back here in two minutes if you hadn't shown up. You come when I tell you to come.'

'Quiet down,' Gregor insisted. They both turned to the older man. He was staring at them from behind his part-laden work bench. 'We all made it out,' he continued. 'We all live till tomorrow.'

'Like you said,' said Hook, turning back on Stella. 'You're no one's boss.' The two of them glared at each other, breathing hard through their noses like angry dogs. The moment extended, the tension between the two seeming to fill the space of the rotunda, while the noise of heavy breathing once again dominated.

'What's going on?' Jared was standing just outside Stella's gift shop bedroom. He was staring at Vine.

Stella broke off eye contact with Hook and turned to Jared. 'This is Vine. He helped us today. He's going to be joining us.'

Jared stared at Vine for a long moment. The angel allowed the attention, implacable under the other man's gaze. 'Okay,' said Jared.

Stella nodded.

'Sleeping in the day time, Captain?' said Hook. 'You feeling okay?'

'I'm getting there. Don't think I realised how tired I was.' Jared's eyes were shadows within shadows, like pools in a forgotten basement suddenly reflecting the tiniest amount of light.

'You've had a long apocalypse,' said Stella. 'End of the world'll take it out of you.'

Jared just nodded. He turned to Gregor. 'Thanks,' he said.

Gregor just grunted and concentrated even more fiercely on his work. 'You should rest,' he said without looking up. 'You're no use to us weak.'

'He's right,' said Stella. 'Get some rest. We'll wake you when it's time to eat and then you can rest some more. And then we'll see about a shower.'

Jared's eyes widened. 'Shower?'

'All in good time,' said Stella. 'For now, rest.'

Jared nodded and walked away, shuffling his feet like a dead.

Stella turned to Vine. 'Any of this any use to you?' she said, gesturing to the angel parts.

'It's unlikely that there'll be nothing I can use. But don't use your parts on me. I've been well maintained by Tash - she's a handy bio-mech. Knows a lot about tech as well.'

'Yeah?' said Gregor, looking up. 'Who'd she work for?'

'No team,' said Vine. 'I think her brother had something to with the Lynxes. She helped out, learned what she could, added it to her IT skills.'

'Polish?' said Gregor.

Vine nodded.

'Sounds too good to be true,' said Gregor.

'Usually that means it is,' said Hook.

'Sounds like someone who will help us,' said Stella. 'Gregor, you could use the help, and Hook, your flesh needs a bit of TLC. You've been smellier than ever this last week.'

Hook shrugged. 'Job gets done. Don't see how smelling nice when you do it makes any difference.'

'It does,' said Stella with a finality that stopped Hook's retort.

An hour later, Stella and Vine were ready to go. They had eaten together but without Jared; everyone had agreed that he needed rest more than canned food. Hook and Stella did not say a word to each other. Vine's appetite was immense and Gregor had commented that it was like having five new mouths to feed. Stella had waved this away, certain that Vine would be able to contribute more than he would take, adding that Hook ate just as much and that her own meals were far from small. Gregor had simply stated that that made his point. Vine took it all in and showed no outward sign of offence.

'I'm sorry about Gregor and Hook,' said Stella. They were walking the streets outside of the Victoria and Albert. It was still quiet as most of the deads in the area would be in Egerton Gardens. 'And I'm sorry you had to see me and Hook's little discussion. We need to blow off steam every now and then.' Stella had her tanto blade strapped to her thigh and Vine carried the two and a half metre bone from the Natural History Museum's blue whale. Stella continued. 'It's been just the three of us for so long that I don't think too much before I speak to them, especially Hook. And with Jared yesterday and you today, it's been a lot to get used to.'

'Don't worry about me, Stella,' said Vine. 'I know that I can contribute to the group, and that once Hook and Gregor get used to me everything will be fine.' He shrugged his massive metal suit. 'Why wouldn't it be? It wouldn't make sense to not have me around.'

Stella stared up at him. 'How much of you is left after the conversion?' she said.

'What do you mean?'

'How much of Michael Vine is still there when the machine gets bolted on?'

'All of him. All of me,' he corrected himself.

'Well, maybe you've forgotten just how much sense some people have. Especially men.'

'Gender has nothing to do with it. We're trying to survive. My inclusion in the group gives us all a much greater chance.'

Stella nodded. 'Very true and very sensible. Let's hope that sense prevails.'

Stella the Zombie Killer Part Twelve

'Where are all the flies?' said Stella to Vine. The two of them strode confidently, even aggressively through London's deserted streets. She walked fast to work out her frustrations with Hook, the argument with him simmering in her brain. Finding Vine's friend Tash was an excellent excuse to get away from the confines of the Victoria and Albert.

'No idea,' said Vine. He looked to the dead vehicles, cars, vans, a police car, an ice cream truck that formed a rusty tunnel of decay. 'When the music plays the ice cream has sold out,' said Vine. 'It's what my mum used to say when the ice cream truck came down our street,' he said in response to Stella's raised eyebrows.

Stella smiled. 'Bet my mum wished she'd thought of that.'

'Bugged her for frozen treats, did you?'

'Yeah. There was always some kind of reward after every class. In the summer it was ice cream.'

'Class?'

'Dance classes, gymnastic classes, karate classes, tennis classes, cricket classes, piano lessons, my parents always kept me busy.'

'How come everything is a class but piano is a lesson?'

Stella stared at Vine, slightly annoyed at her slip. She hadn't realised she had said it. She shrugged. 'Only one I was no good at, I suppose.'

'You were good at cricket?'

'How about you?' said Stella, smoothly avoiding the question. 'How was your childhood filled?'

'Estate gangs and empty ice cream cones.'

Stella glanced at the angel, thought better of questioning him further.

They walked on, the aggression in Stella's stride fading with every step while Vine continued in the exact stride he had employed since they had left the Victoria and Albert.

Looking over the derelict vehicles, she realised she hadn't taken any notice of what they had once been, only seeing them as hiding places behind which danger could lurk. 'Why does danger always *lurk*?' she said, changing the subject for the second time in as many minutes.

Vine glanced at her, amusement evident in his face. 'Because it sounds creepier. More monstrous.'

Stella looked the battered, once gleaming cyborg up and down. 'You're pretty monstrous, but I can't see you lurking.'

Vine grinned. 'No, I suppose I would loom or tower.'

'You're a good size for a bit of looming,' Stella agreed. 'You make Hook look small.'

'I'm no threat to him. I can't hurt him.'

'So you tell us.'

Vine shrugged. 'No way to find out for sure except letting you all beat me to death.'

'Kinda defeats the purpose, I suppose. And I was so looking forward to a little extra-curricular beating,' said Stella, sighing dramatically.

'I'm sure Hook would volunteer.'

Stella laughed ruefully. 'Don't worry about Hook. We have a periodic need to blow off some steam and then have a couple of days' sulking. We'll be back to the Good Life, hoeing and sorting out the chickens before you know it.'

'Chickens?'

'Yeah, we're pretty much self-sufficient. Or at least we've extended the tin can store by about 100 years.'

'Impressive.'

She shrugged. 'Just survival.'

'If it was just survival there'd be a few more of us,' Vine pointed out.

Before she could respond, Stella jerked her head to the left; a noise, movement, a dead struggling through a shattered doorway.

'Allow me.' Vine hefted his huge whale bone, surged at the dead and caved in its skull with the club end. The blow smacked its head to a ninety degree angle before fell to a sudden heap on the path, as if it had been switched off rather than killed.

They stood over the creature for a moment; a ragged pile of bony rotten flesh. 'Flies,' said Stella. 'There should be flies.'

Hook paced the rotunda, while Gregor, still shaken from his excursion, pretended not to notice. 'I'll do an inventory,' said Hook. 'Like you say, lots of new mouths to feed.' He stalked from the rotunda, through an exhibit room now filled with fuel canisters. They had drained the vehicles of their petrol and diesel not long after the crash and used it to fuel the generators in the first long winter, the perpetual dark reducing the solar panels' effectiveness, but the noise had attracted the deads in large numbers. Those early months had been vital lessons in dealing with the deads; the most efficient ways of killing and disposing of them. At first they had tried to bury them but that had quickly become impractical. And so lots of bonfires. Remember, remember the fifth of November, they had said every night, November or not.

But that hadn't lasted. As the zombie angels' numbers grew and the need to hide from the sound of jet packs became an almost daily occurrence the fires had had to stop; angels reacted to flames. They came to put them out. And then their lasers would turn on whoever they saw. In the end they'd retreated inside Vic's, only venturing out when Stella had placed thumpers and the area was cleared. Any bodies they bothered to deal with now were simply stacked in side streets downwind of Vic's.

With generators and fires ruled out it was solar power that had eventually saved their lives, Hook reflected as he entered what had been the Raphael Cartoons, a huge arched room filled now with freezers, the priceless paintings obscured by the towers of freezer cabinets taken from shops and homes. Many of them were of clear glass and Hook smiled, as he always did, to see them so full. A wheeled ladder, liberated from the library, stood waiting to allow access to the second tier of freezers. He remembered his earlier promise about preparing dinner and made a mental note to come back for some diced beef. In the middle of the room were three rows of chest freezers, forming two aisles that were a picture from the past; an image from a frozen food store. As long as you don't look up to the room in which they're housed, he mused.

Cables snaked across the floor, all running from the rotunda where Gregor controlled the flow of power from the solar panels that covered the roofs of Vic's. It had been a frustrating but fruitful task to rip the panelling from nearby buildings; the freezers accounted for around 90% of the power generated by the original panels. The new panels meant that they could still power the freezers and heat enough rooms to live with some comfort in the winter.

Jared's frazzled, haggard face slipped into Hook's mind, and he realised that life could have been a lot harder than shifting a few freezers and solar panels.

Although there were always challenges. He remembered one incident in a Waitrose when he had been too easily distracted by tubs of still-frozen ice cream, the shop's own solar panelling having preserved the pudding. He had been trying to think of ways of getting the freezer and its contents to Vic's as quickly as possible when a hand had touched his shoulder, just lightly at first and then the grip tightening. It was still early in the apocalypse and Hook had been monetarily frozen with fear, just a second, but a second was enough. He had felt the thing's mouth closing on him.

And then there was nothing as the hand was whipped away, the dead crushed by a falling freezer cabinet. When he had looked around Stella stood in the gap left by the knocked over freezer. He had sighed with relief and smiled at her. 'Great, Chewy, always thinking with your stomach,' she had said to him. Hook liked that she knew quotes from movies. Stella never spoke about herself, never opened up and the quotes made it easier to talk to her.

Talking had never been easy with Stella, even in the Games. For five years she had dominated. She was the Games. Hook stopped and glanced at his reflection in the freezer door. He realised that he had no idea what she had done before the Games, when the world was normal and people had worried about their jobs and their mobile phones.

And then the Message came, not to presidents or governments, but to everyone all at once. It was a promise, lots of promises, too good to be true. Or so everyone was told. It took months for it to be listened to seriously; nearly every government in the world denied it: four million lives on four city-sized space ships and one request for asylum. Four million asylum seekers who would bring the world into a new future, one that would eradicate poverty and hunger and disease.

The first promise was to solve the Earth's energy problems. That was free, they said. Plans for super-efficient and easily built solar panelling were sent to every Facebook page, every Twitter account, every email address, every mobile phone. The information was everywhere; no one could own it, everyone could use it.

It was a revolution. Bloodless and clean. But a revolution nonetheless.

After that the governments couldn't keep a lid on the possibilities or the excitement anymore. They couldn't tell their citizens that it was too good to be true because it was already true. Within the first year people's reliance on oil and gas was almost gone. The BRIC nations, Brazil, Russia, India and China moved fastest, wanting to outpace the West. The US, UK and Western Europe lagged behind at first but quickly moved to catch up. How could they not?

Hook had struggled to follow any of it, but he knew that everything was going to be better, knew it, like it was already happening.

The Message was from a species that called itself the Community. They wanted a unified global response to their request for asylum. Some countries, particularly those in the Asia, Africa and South America, billions of people, were desperate to respond positively, to welcome the Community.

In the end the peace had only come through the threat of violence. The Community hadn't understood us, Hook knew that. They had obviously studied us, knew all about us and our history, but they hadn't really understood us, Hook decided. If they had, they wouldn't have offered the weapons.

Hook remembered the panic when four nations, Mexico, Indonesia, Nigeria and Turkey made an offer to the Community: come live with us, one million in each of our countries. We will give you sanctuary. The Community gave them the weapons. Those four countries took them eagerly. Super-powerful conventional weaponry: lasers, blasters, rail guns, missiles and many others that Hook didn't understand, and all powered by the sun. No pollution in their creation or their use. Wipe out your neighbour and move in. No need to clean up.

Maybe it had been deliberate, Hook mused as he picked up a packet of frozen beef. He grabbed it then because he'd probably forget later. The Community had perhaps thought humans would work together out of fear of each other. The term mutually assured destruction was not invented by them; humans had lived by it since it the end of the Second World War. Maybe the Community thought that was the only way we knew how.

The rest of the world had rushed to offer the Community the same protection in every corner of the planet, anywhere they liked. We were all one big happy family standing at an open door. But everyone had a knife behind their back.

Did the Community know? Whether they did or they didn't, they accepted the offer; the weapon technology was available for all. All governments that is; the Community didn't release that on social media.

The angels were next. The technology to make them was sent in return for the promise to dissolve national armies. This was the final straw for some. In America some states declared their own sovereignty, practically the whole of the western side of the United States had become the New United States overnight, and whole countries joined them in refusing: Israel, Iran, Saudi Arabia and Egypt all refusing resulting in the entire Middle East being fenced off from the rest of the world. The Community had shown how to create the power fences that separated them. Easily switched off and on so that when they decided to join the rest of humanity they would be able to quickly and without the need to dismantle any walls. North Korea's silence meant that a similar fence had been erected around that part of the world. The Community had said it was the best way. The Community had said and we all listened, Hook remembered. Power generators were set up in Libya, Turkey, The Gulf of Aden and Afghanistan to wall in the Middle East, while South Korea, China and Japan had provided the space to do the same for North Korea.

The New USA had been a trickier problem. The USA, Canada and Mexico had agreed to host the power plants needed for a massive wall but they couldn't square it anywhere but Hawaii and that would create a no-go area too big to be practical. Hook remember Hilary Clinton, the US president, ordering the construction of a new island off the western coast of the New USA. It almost started a war. The NUSA had threatened to destroy any ships sent to complete the work. In the end agreements were signed and Corner Island was built fifty miles off the coast of Eureka in California. The headlines for the agreement had written themselves. Hook hadn't followed it closely but it had something to do with keeping trade routes open between the old and new USAs.

He had no idea if these areas were still separated. They had been, right up to the crash.

And that was the Message, the promise, that if Earth could unite it would be forever perfect and the angels would look after everyone. It didn't seem much of a unification to Hook, if places could be just fenced off and forgotten about. But that hadn't seemed to matter; it was too good an offer to refuse.

But that was before the crash. The four crashes.

Trust, Hook thought to himself. It was something he and Stella had struggled with since the beginning of all this. And it was trust, or the lack of it, that had ended the promise, ended the dream.

There had been no way to decommission the nukes, at least not safely, not quickly. The Community had agreed to allow their continued presence and the Earth, for it was united now, had promised to begin their disposal. The Community, when they arrived, would be able to speed up the process. They weren't speedy enough.

Hook moved into the cafeteria's kitchen and threw the frozen meat onto the large wooden table. Its impact was loud in the steel room. This room was their fresh food store; vegetables from the garden, eggs and the occasional chicken or rabbit. Most of their protein still came from tin cans and frozen meat and meals, but the garden was Hook's best place. They couldn't grow anything for the first year, the dust in the atmosphere too thick. No sun for a whole year. No wonder so many had died. And once they'd died they made more of themselves till the deads were nearly all that was left. Hook shook the thoughts from his head. He turned to the steel shelf groaning from the weight of the books, his collection of horticultural volumes, salvaged from various shops; he had read them all avidly and now the garden could sustain them indefinitely. And with one addition they wouldn't need tin cans anymore.

Hook dreamed of pigs and that dream always chased away melancholy thoughts of the Message and the crash. He had also read books on keeping livestock and the chapters on pigs were inspirational.

You could do a lot with a pig.

'Ants,' said Vine. He was crouching low over a corpse. They had walked on from their previous encounter and were studying another pile of bones and rags on a garage forecourt. Once-new cars formed two ranks of dusty multi-coloured metal and dirty windscreens, their price signs long since faded.

'What?' said Stella. She was scanning the area, her eyes never still as she looked all around them. The tanker lorry blocking her view of the street worried her. It was dark, cast in shadow by the afternoon sun, making it seem like a wall rather than a vehicle. Pulling her attention away from the truck, she looked down at the dead. It had been killed recently, its skull still leaking fluid from a precise blow with a pointed weapon. Probably an ice pick, Stella thought to herself. That meant people. Living people. She remembered the faces on the phone's screen

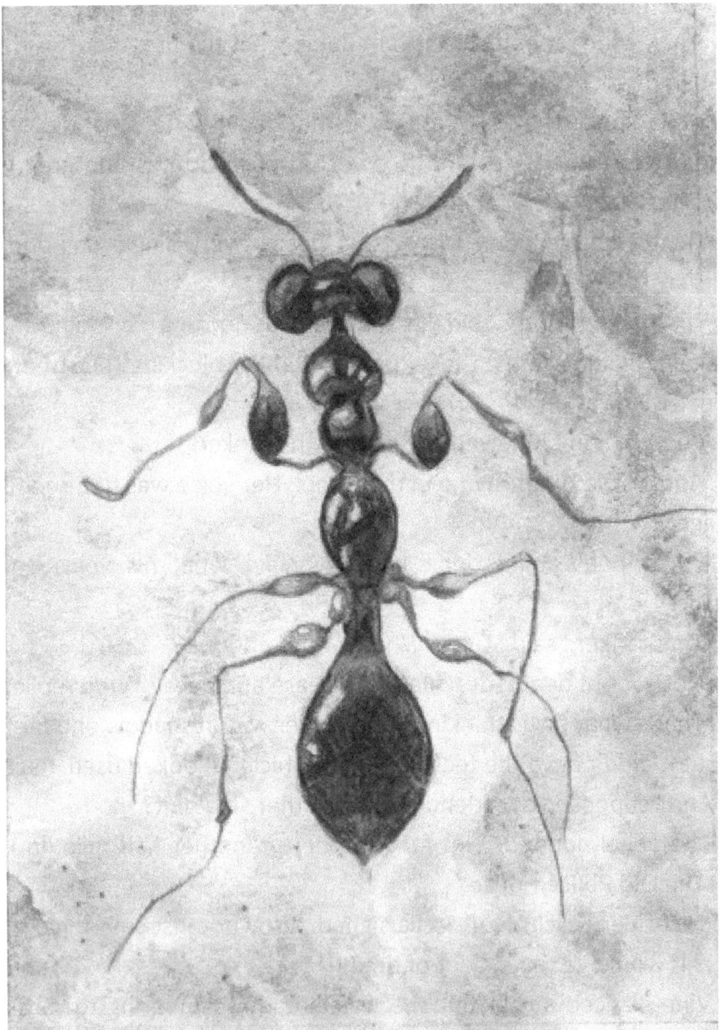

saver and imagined the man and woman, back to back, each carrying an ice pick like post-apocalyptic Charlie's Angels.

'Ants,' Vine repeated. 'Ants are doing what the flies did. This thing's covered in them.'

Stella looked more closely at the body; Vine was right, ants swarmed over the creases and folds of tattered clothes and grey flesh. 'Gross,' she said.

'Death, destruction, disease and decay every single day and you call ants gross.'

'Nice alliteration,' said Stella. She was looking carefully around them again. Buildings on either side and a tanker blocking the street. The only clear way was back.

'I do try.' Vine followed her eyes to the tanker.

'And a little bit of rhyme in there too.' Her voice was flat, seemingly unengaged.

'I'm a poet and I don't know it,' said Vine, his voice equally deadpan.

'That tanker,' said Stella. 'What's weird about it?'

'Not a lot of death, destruction, disease and decay,' Vine replied.

'That's what I was thinking.' The tanker was in shadow and far from clean but it didn't have the feel of a dead vehicle. It looked used. Recently used. 'And I suppose your friend is on the other side of it?

The angel nodded. 'Not far from here. Another half mile, in Hyde Park at the Old Police House.'

'Nice! Very exclusive!' Stella sighed. 'Why not just set up next door to Vic's? It would've saved a lot of time.'

Vine glanced at her but she was already scampering towards the lorry, hugging the buildings for cover. Not used to Stella's impulsive ways, he silently cursed. He couldn't follow her, at least not quietly and so he stood and watched her approach, ready to move if needed.

Stella dodged behind the rear of the tanker and then ran hard at the cab, covering the full length of the truck in a couple of seconds. The metal steps rang to the sound of her heavy boots as she leapt up and hauled open the door.

Empty.

She climbed inside. The seats' upholstery was worn but not neglected. The keys were still in the ignition. Leaning out of the window, she called to Vine. 'Know how to drive a lorry?'

Vine walked over to her, his heavy tread even louder in the open square made by the truck and the buildings. As he approached, he saw shadows moving beneath the cab. 'Stella!' he called.

She heard the urgency in his voice and grabbed the keys, pushed the door open and leapt down to the ground in one fluid movement. Rolling as she hit the dirt, she got a look under the cab and saw the moving shadows. Immediately, she was back on her feet and jogging to Vine. They retreated to the relative shelter of the two rows of cars. Stella squinting at the shadows, trying to gauge numbers, pace of movement, but they were too far away.

'Zombies,' said Vine. He was staring hard, using his ocular array, the blue eye flickering. 'Deads as you call them. Lots of them and more and more all the time.' As he said it a dead spilled from around the front of the cab, catching its shoulder on the grill and jerking to its left before stumbling on again. The material of its jacket torn at the shoulder.

'What's bringing them this way?' said Stella.

Vine shrugged before Stella tapped the metal side of his head. He looked at her, confused and irritated.

'Hey, metal man,' she said. 'What about that scan thing you do? Any thumpers or the like set up near here?'

'Please don't do that,' said Vine. 'It's rude.'

'Sorry,' said Stella, remembering her own annoyance at Hook for snapping his fingers in her face. 'But could you? Would you? Please?'

Annoyance still hardened his face, but he nodded. 'Scanning,' he said. His shining electronic eye swam a little as it moved through differing shades of blue. 'One device set up near here. Just locating. It's five metres that way.' He pointed at the garage's office.

Stella stared at the large windows. There was a desk, a calendar on the wall, its corners curling. No semi naked girls. Lads' version must be in the back, she thought.

'It's powerful,' said Vine. 'More so than the thumpers you use. What kind of range did you get from them?'

'Not far,' said Stella. 'Not much more than a few streets. We just use them to clear a small area.'

'This one will do more than that. It'll call deads in from at least a mile away.'

'A mile? That'd cover Vic's from here. A mile radius. Eight million deads in London. That means...' she didn't finish her sentence.

'Several hundred thousand converging on this point,' said Vine.

'Where is it?' she said, staring at the office. 'Be precise.'

Vine glanced over at the deads trickling around the lorry. There were a couple of dozen already. 'We should leave,' he said.

'Not before we take out the thumper.' Stella's eyes were hard, her face determined, her mouth a thin line.

'It's already too late. The deads will be following the signal. Vic's could already be surrounded.'

'It's never too late.'

Stella the Zombie Killer Part Thirteen

Jared's eyes flicked open. The nightmares receded, the glare of the lasers faded, the faces of old friends grew smaller, the cries of pain quietened. The cries for help he just tried to ignore, but he knew he would never sleep so long again.

'What's happening?' he said to Gregor. He had shuffled through to the rotunda, a blanket wrapped around his shoulders.

Gregor looked up from the angels' parts on his workbench and shrugged. 'Not much. Stella and Vine are out to get another refugee and Hook's sulking.'

'About what?'

'The usual.'

'Stella,' said Jared, nodding. The Cynosure was at the centre of everything.

'They've been like it since the start.'

'You okay?' Jared could see the older man's hands were shaking.

'Had a trip out,' said Gregor, trying to shrug it off and failing. 'Didn't go too well.'

Jared nodded, not knowing what to say, so said nothing. He let his gaze rise away from Gregor, who had bent his head back to his work. Jared stared at the blue and green of the chandelier. The afternoon, he assumed it was the afternoon, sunlight flooded through it, seeming to move the chandelier as it burned its course as a flashing stream of chemical flames.

He looked away, reminded as he was of the previous day and his attempt to stare at the sun, to burn his vision and eradicate the memory of his group's final moments. But he was lost, lost then and lost now, suddenly living with people that he didn't know.

Sean's face rose to fill his vision and he swayed on the spot, a heavy weight and dizziness spreading through him, making his body feel like a diseased tree ready to fall. Sean's face, dogged, strong, so alive, so alert.

So dead. Sean had been Jared's reason for so long that he hadn't ever allowed himself to see it, had never cared to admit it.

Jared didn't fall. His right foot shot back and planted firmly on the tiled floor, his knees bent, but held. He looked at Gregor, who nodded approvingly at him, and let the blanket slip to his elbows. Balling it, he walked into the desk's circle and sat next to the other man, dropping the blanket on a spare shelf beneath the desk. 'Can I help?' he said. 'I never got that close to the angels but I might know a few things.'

'Help yourself,' said Gregor, spreading his arms along the piles of parts. 'I need ocular parts for Stella's eyes and Hook's back support is failing - though he won't admit it.'

Jared looked carefully among the components, knowing that Gregor could find the pieces easily on his own, but grateful for the chance to help. 'What does she need?'

'Night vision. Zoom'd be useful but not essential.'

'Two?'

'Just one. She's half and half in the eye department.'

Jared nodded. He searched through the ocular spares, discarding anything that was too blue, too robotic.

Gregor saw what he was doing. 'Beggars can't be choosers,' he said. 'If she ends up with a blue eye, she ends up with a blue eye.'

'Okay,' Jared nodded. 'Then there's plenty to work with. There are targeters too. Would she want those?'

Gregor shrugged. 'She's never been one to use guns. And I don't know how we'd link it to anything we could get hold of anyway. They're designed for the angels' arm lasers.'

'Better to have it and not need it than to need it and not have it?'

Gregor nodded. 'I'll ask her. She's practical. She'll take it.'

'How long have you been looking after her?'

'Three years before the crash and ever since. Six years in all.' Gregor was nodding, his face flushed with pride, his hands no longer shaking.

'How'd she take it? The crash I mean.'

Gregor shrugged. 'The same as everyone else.'

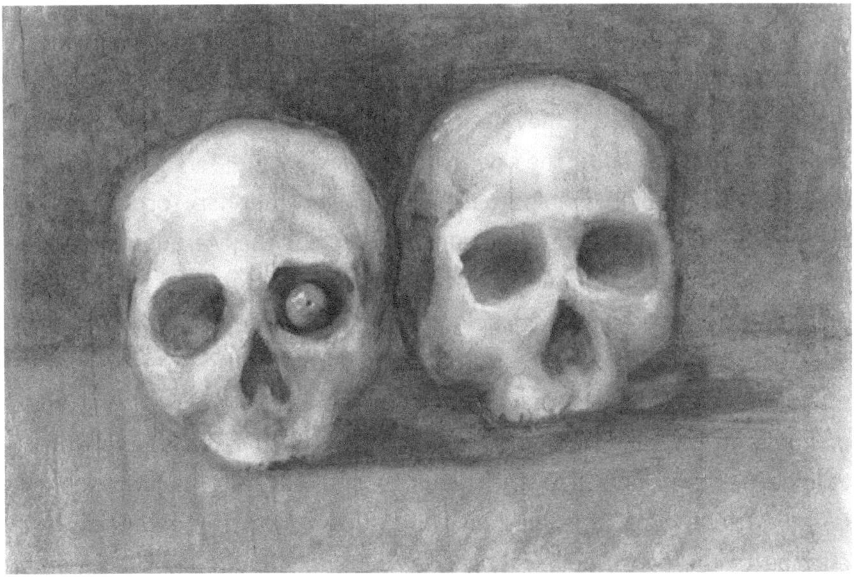

Jared nodded. To call the crash a disappointment was missing the point of just how much it meant to everybody. It was a tragedy for the entire planet. The promise of a secure and happy future gone in those eight minutes.

Not the entire planet; someone had launched those missiles. Individuals or governments, it didn't really matter; the promise was dead. Three launched in unison, one from the NUSA, one from Israel and one from Australia. That had been a shock. The Australians had never admitted to possessing nuclear weapons. Jared remembered the TV journalists frantically discussing the possibility of Australia launching of its own accord or if terrorists had used the country as a launch pad. If the latter was true, how did they get the nuke into the country? Not that it mattered. They talked till the skies turned black.

The Community's ships had entered geostationary orbits above each of the poles, the Central African Republic and the Marquesas Islands in the Pacific Ocean. No one had ever heard of it before the Community arrived. It was special only for being on the other side of the world from the Central African Republic. Its tourist industry flourished to the point that there was a fifteen-year waiting list for every hotel, existing and planned, on the islands. The NUSA had taken out the ship at the North Pole, Israel the Central African Republic and Australia the Marquesas Islands. Three ships consumed in white nuclear fire. Three wrecks that crashed to the earth, obliterating everything for hundreds of miles and throwing up so much dust and ash and debris into the atmosphere that the sun wasn't seen for a year.

The world had watched. Worst of all, the ships had been broadcasting on social media. They hadn't revealed their physical bodies as yet but they had communicated ever since they had first made contact. Most humans had members of the Community on their friends and followers lists.

They read their final words. They heard them die. The ships had no defence against a nuclear attack. Why would they when their approach had been agreed for years.

And then the fourth had launched.

That came from the UK, or at least from a Trident submarine, no one knew which one, lurking beneath the waves. It took out the final ship orbiting above the South Pole. The sub must have been in Antarctic waters.

Ridiculously, one news channel had raised a scientist working in Antarctica. She couldn't tell them anything. She was scared. Ignored for the last five years, her work so terrestrial when everything was about the extra terrestrial, and now they put her on the TV, a terrified face watching the clouds as the first three crashes covered the sun, the life, the hope. Three crashes and a fourth about to hit her. It was compulsive viewing. Jared had watched with his colleagues in Angel Control. No one had said a word. No one had seen the fourth hit; the debris, the ash, had started its long winter.

Gregor was staring at him.

'What?' said Jared. He was separating lenses from their white housing.

'You stink.' Gregor's voice was flat but not unkind. 'You should shower. It's over there.' He nodded to the main entrance. Jared remembered the cloakrooms to either side.

'A working shower?'

Gregor nodded. 'We usually limit ourselves to thirty seconds but in your case...' he looked Jared up and down. 'Take as long as you need.'

Jared stared through the arch to the main entrance.

'It won't bite,' said Gregor. 'There are clean clothes. You can ditch the ones you're wearing; we're well stocked.'

'Thank you,' said Jared as he rose from his seat. He was nervous, ridiculously so.

'And there's a razor in there as well,' said Gregor. He waved a hand at Jared's face. 'We can see what's underneath all that hair.'

'The shower, is it rain water?'

Gregor laughed. 'It's not exactly a power shower but it's more than just a watering can. Solar powered water reclamation and recycling machine. We nicked it from Buckingham Palace when we still had a working van.'

Jared gaped. 'You went to the palace?'

'Yeah,' said Gregor casually. 'Kicked some undead royal ass, got the plumbing and legged it. The queen was hard to put down with all those zombie corgis going for our ankles.'

'You're teasing me,' said Jared.

Gregor just shrugged. 'Why is it any less believable than anything else that's happened since all this started?'

Jared stared at the man's impassive face and returned the shrug. 'Huh,' he said. He turned to walk through the huge arch.

Once Jared's back was turned, Gregor smiled then bent his head to his work.

Stella the Zombie Killer Part Fourteen

'I can't leave Tash!' Vine shouted to Stella as she ran for the garage office.

'You go to your people, I go to mine,' she shouted over her shoulder.

'But what if there are too many?'

'I'll take care of it. We have a plan for this sort of thing. Go!'

Deads had cascaded around the tanker that blocked the road and they had filled the street outside of the garage. Vine hadn't been so close to so many since the early days after the crash when solar power had been hard to come by. He glanced once more at Stella and made up his mind; he would clear a space for her and then get to Tash as quickly as he could.

Stella burst into the office, throwing a glance over her shoulder at Vine as he weighed into the deads, his massive weapon swinging and clubbing the staggering horde back. She knew that he wouldn't wait for her but she was grateful for the valuable minutes he was buying her.

The office was sparse, the plain dark wood desk empty. Looted, Stella presumed, although what could be taken she had no idea. The calendar was open at August 2020, exactly three years ago. Its owner had circled the 20th. A birthday? An anniversary? Something too important to forget. 'Dates don't matter anymore,' she said out loud. Then she shrugged. 'Except Christmas.'

She quickly searched the room for a thumper-type device. It sat on the floor behind the desk, not in plain sight but certainly not hidden. It was larger than the thumpers she and Hook used and looked to be solar charged. She briefly considered taking it for Gregor to study but rejected the idea; it would be too risky to try to carry it through a horde.

The sound of a launching jet pack told her that Vine had gone. She glanced through the office window and saw that the deads had been forced back to the tanker truck. 'Thanks, metal man,' she said, and turned to kick the thumper. It smashed easily but she stamped on it some more, grinding the parts beneath her heel to ensure that the signal was killed.

If Hook and Gregor were keeping watch on the street then they would be awaiting her return. That way the emergency re-entry plan, or the ERP as Hook called it, would swing into action. Stella tried to imagine Hook swinging into anything. She couldn't but she could certainly imagine him battering into things and that would be just as good.

Adrenaline coursed through her body, working its magic. She liked to think of it as magic rather than bio-mechanically enhanced adrenal glands; the latter sounding so clinical. And of course, no one knew the long term effects of such enhancement. She was about as long term as it got and she still felt fine, better than fine, magical. Magic was easier to deal with than biology.

She leapt over the desk and was already sprinting at full speed before she reached the rows of cars. Her tanto blade didn't slow her at all and she silently cursed herself for going out so often unarmed.

She was only a three-minute run from Vic's but she had no idea how long the thumper had been transmitting; there could be hundreds of deads there by now and she would have no way of getting back inside. Well, there was one way: Gregor's Emergency Re-entry Plan, or ERP for short. But the plan only worked if they could communicate and for that she needed the thumper tracker. She could see it now on the desk in the concourse. 'I'll think of something,' she said to herself.

Jared let the water fall over him, smoothing it through his hair, down his body, around every part of him, feeling the grime beneath his fingers as it was rinsed away. His toes splashed in the brown water like potatoes poking from muddy earth. His beard was as much of a tangle as his hair and he could smell the water as it gushed through it. It didn't smell nice.

There was shower gel. At first he had stared at it, the water running off his lashes, obscuring the bright red bottle. He hadn't used soap in three years. Then he grabbed it and filled his palm till it overflowed. It smelled of strawberries. He scrubbed it into his body over and over. He grabbed the bottle and filled his palm again, this time lathering his hair, using his fingers to pull at the tangles and the knots. He pulled and rubbed hard enough to hurt, pulling hair from his scalp and knocking scabs and scars on his body.

The pain was like an elation to him. He pulled and rubbed and massaged at his hair and bruised flesh. At one point he had to reach down and clear the plughole of hair and filth to allow the water to flow.

When he was out, he poured more hot water into a sink and grabbed scissors and a razor. He attacked the hair around his face, thought about doing the same for that on his head, but decided against it, and snipped until he thought he could trim the rest.

He wiped steam from the mirror and watched as he swiped the electric beard trimmer across his chin. He switched to a wet razor and carved a tidy beard from the mess on his cheeks, revealing pink skin. He stared at it. He hadn't seen anything but weathered, red and grey flesh in so long.

He looked back to the shower and smiled. He jumped back in.

The water ran cold after two minutes and the power dipped as the machine struggled to keep up, but it didn't matter. Jared stood there for as long as he could stand it.

Stella ran on, her boots pounding the debris strewn streets. The deads at the garage were no longer a concern, only what was between her and Vic's. She had already taken out a few of the shufflers and even a couple of draggers that had pulled themselves from buildings and vehicles. Bits of their flesh stuck to her black vest and black combats. She glanced at the clear blue sky, hoping there was enough power for a shower, not considering if she would be alive to use it.

A dead stumbled out from behind the ice cream van right next to her as she ran past. 'Sorry, fella. In a rush. We'll speak later, yeah?' The dead looked at her, its face blank as it started to follow her. Now that the thumper was disengaged, her open running would attract a lot of unwanted attention. She considered killing each one that she saw instead of just those in the way but she wanted to be back as quickly as possible. The vision of Gregor standing on the steps at Vic's, his ridiculous sword, held impotently in two weak hands, forced her on.

She was running down Queen's Gate; ahead of her a loose mob of deads blocked the way. There were enough to mean that she would have to be careful not to get surrounded, which would mean taking several seconds on each kill. Too long.

Without breaking stride she ran to the broken cars and leapt onto the bonnet of the first, then the roof and then, using the rear windscreen as a springboard, a long leap to the next bonnet, her boots making atrocious noise as metal buckled and windscreens cracked. But she ran on, leaping from one car to the next, every dead head jerking around to face her. Their bodies aligned with their heads like frayed and twisted elastic limply springing back into shape. Soon she had a shambling procession filling the street and aiming itself at her running figure.

But she was ahead of them as she rounded the comer onto Cromwell Road and saw Vic's, dead ahead. Vic's and something else. Some things else. The sight brought her to a skidding halt; deads, hundreds of them. 'Well that's a lot of undead and unwelcome guests,' she said. Glancing around, she saw that several of the deads from Queen's Gate were already nearly on her. 'You know what?' she said, to the closest dead as she batted its arms aside and thrust the tanto through its chin and into its brain. As it fell, she said to it, 'I don't think any of you guys had an invite. Time to leave.'

Suddenly, a hand on her shoulder. She cursed herself for allowing the distraction, turned and thrust her blade into its eye. 'Fair enough,' she said. 'Stakes are high. Time for the big-girl game face.'

The Ismaili Centre was across the road, a large, stark, concrete building with no entrance on this side but lots of large glass windows facing Cromwell Road. She clicked her heels and round-housed a dead, stabbing her blade into the side of its head. She pushed the blade smoothly back into her boot and ran at the closest window. 'Here goes nothing,' she said, and leapt at the glass, shoulder first, tucking her head into the crook of her arm.

She bounced off.

Tash watched from the window as Vine landed softly in the Old Police House's courtyard, right next to the green tractor left behind by dead park keepers. His descent was so graceful for such a large man. If it wasn't for the whine of the jet pack, he really could have been an angel descending from heaven, Tash thought as she watched him. She didn't mind that the sound had attracted a few zombies; the park's trickle of shuffling corpses had become a flood in the last twenty minutes, but that was to be expected. The double-glazed windows of the grand old house could withstand a few pawing palms and she had already closed all of the curtains, so they would lose interest soon enough.

She smoothed her blonde hair, cropped short to avoid grasping hands, away from her forehead and went out to meet him. Dust and dirt and grime covered everything in the courtyard; the space was shut off from the rest of the park so the rains had failed to wash away much of the fallout from the crash. Vegetation, most of it domestic but some less so, its seeds fetched up into the atmosphere and then dumped again far from home, grew everywhere, like a creeping green and yellow creature trying to escape the courtyard and pull down the building in its passing. Despite the mess Tash walked confidently, her feet comfortable in a brand new pair of red Converse, her legs wrapped in brand new jeans, topped off with a bright white t-shirt with a Community logo emblazoned across her chest in green.

'Welcome back,' she said to Vine.

'The clothes look good,' he said.

She smiled warmly. 'Thanks. What's that?' She pointed at the huge weapon his hands.

'A whale bone. It's been very useful.'

Stains of blood and gore decorated either end of the bone. 'Certainly looks useful,' she said. 'How did it go with the Cynosure and her friends?'

'Very well,' he answered. 'They've set up quite an operation in that museum; we'll be able to use much of what they have.'

Tash nodded. 'And the bio-mech, he was there?'

'Just like you predicted. It's Gregor.'

'I knew it. There was no way that the Cynosure and Hook could have kept going this long without someone propping them up. Those Games athletes are nothing without their maintenance.' Tash pursed her lips thoughtfully before continuing. 'And Gregor! He was the best. That means he'll have all sorts of tech we can use. It'll be a safe bet that he's got equipment that we haven't seen since the crash. Just the kind of equipment we need.'

'His work space was hard to assess because of the angel parts, but it certainly looked well-equipped.'

Tash nodded eagerly. 'This is it then. They're going to be holed up in that building for at least a week once the zombies get around them. That's a week to get you sorted and then we can go to Kyle.'

'They call them deads,' said Vine.

'A good name,' said Tash, nodding again. She was excited. The plan would work.

'We'll have to wait till tomorrow,' said Vine. 'I need to charge.'

'Go ahead. We're safe here. The zombies, the deads, will make sure no one can get in. Rest now and tomorrow we'll go be the perfect house guests.' She left Vine alone in the courtyard and returned the house. She watched him from a window. He had climbed to the roof of the green tractor and was just spreading his golden wings, turning the courtyard into a bowl of sunlight so thick it was like liquid. Like a fuel, she thought to herself.

Tomorrow. She made the silent promise to herself, to her brother and to Kyle.

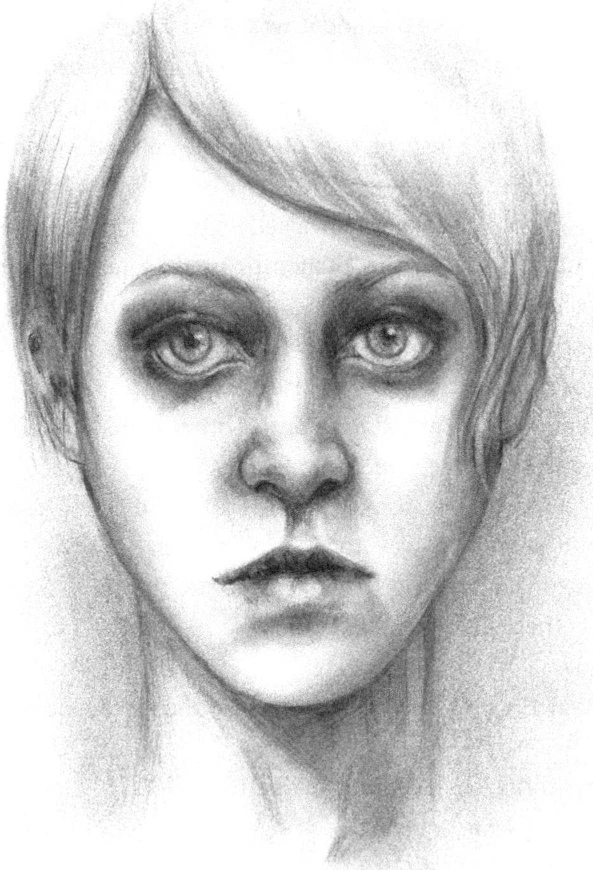

Stella the Zombie Killer Part Fifteen

Hook strolled back through the freezer room, swinging his bag of diced beef and a cabbage from his left hand, potatoes and carrots from the other. He had herbs in the rotunda. Cooking was easier there, the kitchen too far away from anywhere, and it was good to be together as much as possible; remind each other that not everyone was dead. Although, he supposed, now that there were going to be six of them it would be best to either make more use of the kitchen or shift a table down to the rotunda.

'Hey, Gregor,' he said as he walked up to the circular desk. 'What do you think, start eating in the kitchen or move a table through here? I think we should still keep eating together when Robocop and his girlfriend join us.'

Gregor shrugged. 'Up to you. I don't care.'

'Yes you do,' he said, staring at the other man. 'C'mon, Gregor, we can really make this place work for all of us. Maybe we could make more use of the cafeteria.' He paused thoughtfully and then shook his head. 'Suppose it'd still seem way too big even with six of us.' He glanced towards the main entrance and listened to the noise coming there. 'Someone in the shower? Stella back?'

'Jared.'

'Captain JJ's up? How's he doing? He looked deader than a dead earlier.'

Gregor shrugged. 'Seemed a bit better.'

'You know, I was thinking...'

'Steady on.'

'Yeah, thanks,' said Hook sarcastically. 'I was thinking that we haven't had it that bad, you know? When you think what he must've been through, we've done pretty well in comparison.'

Gregor nodded but scowled. 'No one helped us. We earned all this.'

'I know, I know,' said Hook hurriedly. 'I was just taking the time to be thankful, you know?'

'Found some religion in the freezers did you? Is Jesus in the diced beef?' he nodded at the bag in Hook's hand.

'That reminds me.' Hook popped the beef into the microwave and started the defrost function. The oven whirred into life. He looked up and waved his vegetable knife in the direction of the shower. 'How long's he having? Seems a bit longer than thirty seconds.'

'Thought he needed our share,' said Gregor.

'Fair enough,' said Hook. He smiled at Gregor. 'Good idea.'

Gregor returned the look. 'What's up with you?'

At that moment Jared emerged.

The other two gaped at him. He was a different man; face clean and beard trimmed, clean clothes, combats and a loose green shirt, clean hair, still long but combed, and new boots that made him walk with a confident stride.

'Hey, Captain. Feeling better?' Hook asked.

'You've no idea,' Jared replied.

Hook nodded as Jared joined them at the desk. Jared pointed at the ingredients. 'Can we trust his cooking?' he said to Gregor.

'He does okay,' said Gregor.

'Sounds like high praise from you,' said Jared. 'Will there be seconds?' he said to Hook.

'I doubt it,' Hook replied. 'But I'll try to make sure the firsts are first, second and last.'

'That would be marvellous.' Jared smiled. It was a little forced but it was there, like a sign on his face that said, that's it, I'm here now, let's make it work.

Hook looked at Jared and smiled, then waved his hands at the interior of the Victoria and Albert. 'We've got all this stuff...' Hook began.

'Touch some wood,' said Gregor, cutting him off.

'What?'

'You're tempting fate. Touch some wood.'

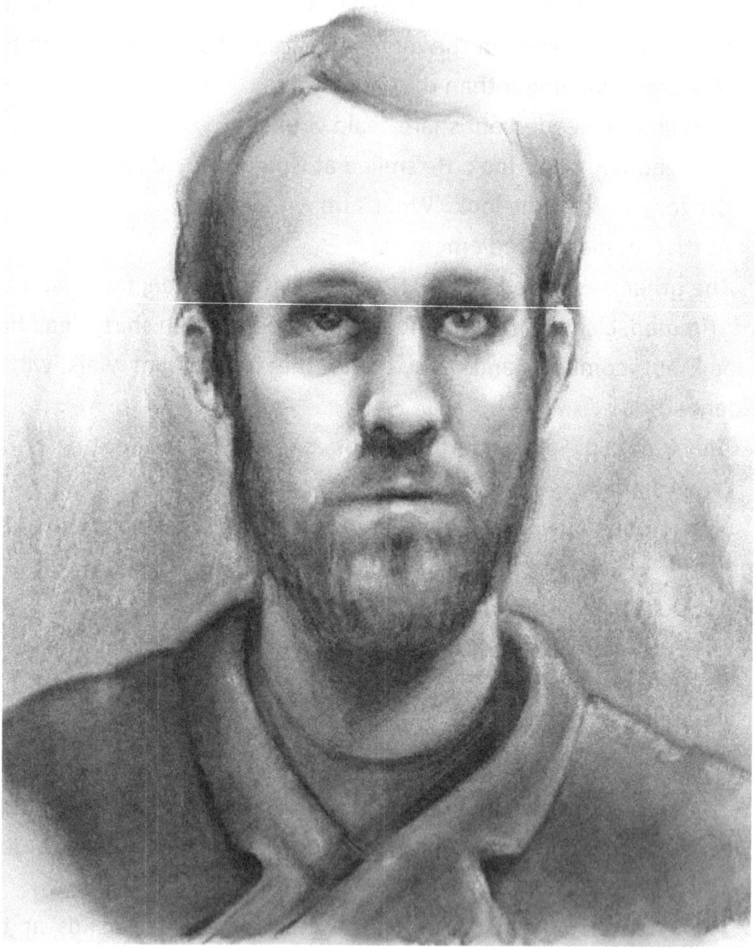

'Who's got religion?' Nevertheless, Hook reached out to touch the wooden desk. 'Touch wood,' he said deliberately. 'We've got all this stuff,' he continued after throwing a will-that-do glance at Gregor, 'and we've got the garden and we've got loads of space. I think Stella's right about saving who we can. We could set up a community here.'

'We can't feed everybody,' said Gregor. He didn't look up from his work with remains of the angels.

'But we could help who we find,' said Hook as earnestly as he could. Even Jared looked up at the tone in his voice. 'Imagine this place full of people, all working together to make things easier. It'd certainly be warmer with a whole community in here during the winter.'

'Not *the* Community though,' said Jared.

'That boat's sailed, I reckon.' Hook set about peeling and chopping, the kitchen utensils tiny in his hands. He glanced over at Gregor and sighed at the sight of the man's bent head. 'Got anything useful?' he asked, nodding at the angels' bits.

'Plenty. Including a back support for you.'

'I don't need it!' Hook protested.

'Don't be a baby. It's for your own good.'

Hook sighed as he finished chopping the potatoes. 'At least I haven't got dodgy eyes like Stella. I couldn't cope with you cutting into my eyes.'

'You would if it was bionic. I just switch it off. You're more likely to feel pain with a back operation.'

Hook groaned. He chopped carrots and threw them into a pan of water, then lit a flame beneath it. The onions were next. Hook turned away from Gregor and Jared so that they wouldn't see him cry.

Stella yelled in pain as she landed with a thud on the ground outside of the Ismaili Centre. Her left shoulder and upper arm had taken the brunt of the fall. A quick glance showed blood and a ragged wound. Quickly ignoring the pain, she rolled away from the nearest dead and staggered to her feet.

'Ow, ow, ow, ow, ow...' She ran to the window again, reaching into her cargo pants pocket for her glass cutter. Blood was running down her left arm and she could feel her left shoulder beginning to seize up. She glared at a dead as if daring it to come closer. It duly did, stumbling at her, its arms raised, She placed the glass cutter into her left palm and retrieved her tanto from her thigh. The blade was into the dead's eye in a heartbeat, but the action meant she was off balance and another dead was able to grab her wounded shoulder. She yelled in pain as its clawed fingernails dug into her flesh, pulling her away from the collapsing dead and almost wrenching the tanto from her hands.

Grimly she held on to the handle of the blade, pulled it from the dead and arced it around to the face of the other. She plunged the blade hilt-deep into its face, missing the eye but powering through the nose and into the brain. The dead dropped like a stone and she fell on top of it, the glass cutter spilling from her numb left hand.

She rolled off the dead, grimacing as fiery pain burned in her shoulder, and tried to reach the glass cutter with her left arm. Another dead lurched for her and she had to roll away, the cutter kicked by the dead as it reached for her.

Looking up, she saw that deads surrounded her, blocking her view. She had no idea which way was which, no idea which way to spin or roll or leap. She looked at the tanto in her hand, the twelve-inch blade dull with blood and gore, and thought of Gregor's sword, wishing she had something like it, something that she could swing in a heavy arc.

'No point in wishing,' she said to the deads and kicked out at legs, breaking bones and shattering kneecaps. She struggled up to her knees, trying to see something other than zombie heads and filthy, reaching hands. Her left arm was almost shot. Thoughts of a break filled her mind, but she pushed the thoughts and the pain down into the long shadows of her mind.

Over the deads' heads she could see the Ismaili Centre to her left, meaning that Vic's was to her right and behind her. She rose smoothly to her feet, already learning to compensate for her left arm, and slashed with her tanto at legs and reaching arms to clear space.

She knew now that she should have stayed with Vine, gone to his friend Tash and waited this out.

Time slowed, the waves of death flowed around her like she was a rock on a beach untouched by the tide but soon to be swallowed. Briefly she considered standing still and letting the swell of rotten flesh overwhelm her. No one would know that it was deliberate; she could just leave this place and the struggle would be done.

The thought was so brief that she barely registered it as she kicked another dead in the face, sending its teeth flying.

Trees stood at the opposite corner, away from Vic's but offering valuable cover. Stella knew that there was an ice rink in those trees, a remnant of yesteryear and the Natural History Museum's attempts to reach out to the young and disinterested.

But she rejected the trees as too far away to get Hook's and Gregor's attention. Stabbing a dead in the face, she looked over towards Vic's, and remembered the phone box, the old style red phone box, just across the road. If she could make it to that she could climb to the roof away from grabbing hands and wait it out, maybe get Hook's or Gregor's attention. Behind the phone box was another stand of trees. They could be used in the ERP

Sighing, she stabbed another dead in the face, careful this not time not to use her full strength and send herself off balance. Another dead received a kick in the kneecap, dropping it so that she could stamp on its head, its skull cracking and squashing in one blow.

The phone box was no more than fifty metres away; a dash along the path, across a short patch of grass and then one road. Fifty metres and a few hundred deads. They weren't too densely packed yet. If she was quick enough, she could exploit the gaps.

She let the adrenaline flood her system again and prepared to run.

Jared looked up from the ocular implant he was preparing as the microwave pinged. He watched as Hook moved smoothly from the vegetables to pull open the door, pull the bag from inside and spread its contents onto a chopping board. He grabbed another onion. 'You've already used an onion,' Jared reminded Hook.

'You can never have too much onion with beef,' said Hook, flourishing his knife.

'Wait,' said Gregor. 'Cooking checks.'

Hook sighed. 'C'mon, Gregor, what would be happening that we didn't know about? There's nothing going on; we'll be okay.'

'Stella's out, Vine's out, we're waiting for someone new. If that's not a recipe for something going wrong, I don't what is.'

'You didn't say disaster,' said Jared.

Hook and Jared stopped what they were doing and stared at Jared, shock plain on their faces.

'What?' said Jared. 'What did I say?'

'We don't use that word,' said Gregor.

'Ever,' Hook added.

'What, 'disaster'?' said Jared.

Hook and Gregor shuddered a little. 'You're new,' said Gregor. 'You don't understand. We'll let it slide.'

'Eh?' said Jared.

'The word,' said Hook. 'It doesn't matter because you didn't know, but we don't use that word. It's bad luck.'

'Okay,' said Jared. 'But you still didn't say that word. I was just curious.'

'We take as few chances as possible,' said Gregor. 'Or at least we used to,' he added with a sigh.

Hook sniggered. 'It used to be me in trouble for being too hot-headed. How things change!' He laughed out loud and then tried to be more serious as he looked at Jared. 'When we're cooking,' he explained, 'we always check for deads to make sure we don't attract too many with the smell,' said Hook.

'Sounds sensible,' said Jared. 'But why worry about dis...'

He was cut off by Hook and Gregor raising their hands in protest,

'Why worry about things going wrong,' Jared corrected himself, 'when you seem to have so many safeguards in place?'

'Because things always go wrong,' said Gregor, shrugging. 'And safeguards are only safeguards if we use them,' he added.

Jared was suddenly serous. 'Too true,' he said.

'Okay!' said Hook, raising his hands in the air in mock submission. 'I'll go check for deads. How about I grab a bottle of wine for Cap's first fresh meal since the apocalypse?' He turned on the other two and winked. 'Now there's a thing you wouldn't have thought you would say five years ago!' He jogged out of the rotunda and towards the freezers.

'Leave the wine!' Gregor called after him.

'You have booze here?' said Jared.

'We do,' said Gregor. 'But we only open it once a week. We have it with movie night.'

'You have a movie night?'

Gregor grimaced. 'All the comforts of home,' he said gruffly.

Jared thought he saw the chandelier move just a little, the blue and green flashes almost seeming to signal something. But he dismissed it.

Stella ducked, dodged, kicked, stabbed and slashed her way through the deads. Even with her wounded arm she was still fast enough to keep the deads from coming together to form an impassable mass. But she was slowing. Drenched in blood and swaying at her hip, her left arm was pretty much useless; the blood loss, the fading adrenaline, the sweat streaming into her eyes. The red phone box was just ahead, its starkly coloured sides bobbing in out of view, like an island on the horizon seen from a boat adrift and helpless, pulled and pushed by waves that were growing.

Hook returned to the rotunda, his face serious. 'Dinner's cancelled,' he said.

'What?' said Gregor. 'What is it?'

'Stella,' Hook replied. 'She's in trouble. He turned to Jared. 'You ever fire a harpoon?'

Jared shook his head. 'No, never.'

'Well,' said Hook. 'There's a first time for everything.'

Stella the Zombie Killer Part Sixteen

'Is that it?' said Jared.

Hook nodded. The two of them stood at a first floor window at the front of the Victoria and Albert Museum. The harpoon launcher was fixed to the floor, its deadly missile pointing out of one of the narrow, arched windows. 'There was a whaling exhibit back in 2018. We found this in storage.'

'What are we gonna do with it?'

'Fire it into the phone box.'

Jared stared out across the street and the hundreds of deads; the phone box was a little to the right and surrounded by deads, as was a figure in combats and a vest fighting them off, its left arm swinging uselessly at its side. 'She's not gonna last much longer.'

'That's why we're rushing, Captain. Pleased to see that you're fully fit again.'

'Right, sorry,' said Jared.

Hook hauled the window open. 'Aim for the middle of the phone box. It'll catch in the frame of the door if it doesn't bury itself in the ground.'

'It'll be a concrete floor!' Jared protested.

'Not a time for discussion, Cap. Get it done.'

'What are you gonna do?'

'Something noisy.'

'Will it pull her back up?' said Jared, nodding at the harpoon.

'It's a harpoon not a Batman grapple gun; she'll have to climb.'

'She'll never make it.'

'You haven't really met Stella properly yet, have you?' said Hook, and he was gone, running down the stairs and back through the freezer room to the main doors.

Jared set himself behind the harpoon and took a few moments to familiarise himself with the weapon. The launcher had been bolted to the floor and could be manipulated to fire from any of three arched windows in the front of Vic's. The missile was already loaded. A trigger sat ready underneath. Not the most complicated weapon Jared had ever fired. He lined it up with the phone box, saw how far Stella still was from it. His eyes flicked back and forth from Stella to the box. He was sweating.

'Whatever you're going to do, Hook, do it now.'

Hook dashed down the stairs, back through the freezer room and into the store of fuel. He grabbed a crate of bottles with rags stuffed into the necks. Molotovs.

'That's not part of the plan!' Gregor shouted as Hook ran into the rotunda. 'You can't use those; you'll have angels swarming all over us if they see a fire. For God's sake, you know better than I do that just standing outside the front door's enough to have all of them swarming over us for days.'

Hook paused at the desk, slamming the bottles of fuel down as he did so. 'What do you suggest I do? Throw some harsh words at them?'

'Trust the plan and trust Stella. You start throwing bombs about and this place is no longer a secret.'

Hook, breathing hard, stared at the other man, his eyes wide, searching for a solution in Gregor's face.

'She'll make it,' said Gregor. 'You know she will.' He placed his hands on the crate.

Stella swept a dead's legs from under it and then stamped on its head, cracking but not crushing its skull. She stamped again, finishing the job. The sweep had been slow, the stamp weak, she knew. Energy levels were falling. Behind her, the Ismaili Building was more than halfway. No point in turning back. A valuable second passed as she tried to calm her breathing. More and more deads were noticing her and the phone box was still twenty metres away.

Two hedges, once low and manicured, now hugely overgrown, offered minimal protection but she dove for them like a drowning woman

offered a raft. The grass was knee high and damp. It smelled of summer, of quiet days and cricket in the park.

Deads followed her, their shabby clothing catching in the privet branches and shattering her illusions. They caught their legs and feet in the green tangle and fell to their knees, the following creatures bowling them onto their faces, their rolling bodies tripping those behind them. Stella was momentarily fascinated at the scrum of deads and how ridiculous they looked, bumping and tumbling as if they were falling off a tiny cliff.

Then she was dashing forward, her boots whipping through the grass, stabbing into heads quickly and efficiently, allowing a wall of corpses to build before her. Within a minute it was a metre high and with the added barrier of the hedges she had a precious few minutes to rest.

'How's she doing, Captain?' said Hook as he jogged back to Jared's position.

'Caught between a rock and hard place,' said Jared, nodding at the hedges. 'She dove in between those. Can't see her now but the deads don't seem to be able to get to where she is. And they seem pretty calm.'

'What do you mean?' said Gregor. He had followed Hook up the stairs.

'If Stella was dead they'd be tearing her body to pieces by now,' said Hook. 'Smell of blood would be driving them mad. As mad as they get anyway.'

Jared nodded.

'So while they're just milling around those hedges we can assume she's alright?' said Gregor.

'That's pretty much it,' said Hook. He turned away from the window and punched the wall behind them with a loud thump.

Jared noticed the cracks form in the plaster.

'That's not going to help,' said Gregor.

'Better than just milling about!' Hook responded loudly.

'Best not to shout,' said Jared. 'You never know who's listening.'

'Yeah, yeah, apocalypse survival one-on-one. Thanks, *Captain*,' said Hook sarcastically.

'I didn't mean anything by it. I've seen too many people act stupid under pressure, that's all,' said Jared.

'Are you calling me stupid? Nice way to make yourself part of the group, JJ!'

'He's right,' said Gregor. 'You are being stupid. Think. Don't punch.'

'Dammit!' Hook turned on the wall again but just stood and seethed with frustration before he turned back on the other two men. 'What the hell are we supposed to do?'

'We wait for her to get to the phone box. That's all we can do,' said Gregor.

The three of them stared out of the window at the overgrown hedges. Minutes passed and deads still surrounded Stella's position. They had started to circle the hedges. Whatever had brought them in this direction was less of a draw than a warm body in a hedge.

'There must be something we can do,' said Hook. 'She wouldn't wait this long if she was okay. You haven't seen her in action like I have. There must be something wrong or she'd be on that box dancing the fandango by now.'

'Adrenaline,' said Gregor. 'With the wound she's maybe run low.'

'Can't rely on adrenaline alone,' said Jared. 'I've seen people get pumped up. Next thing they're just dead. And she's the Cynosure; she must have other skills to fall back on.'

Hook and Gregor both nodded before the older man continued. 'She certainly does but she'll be tired, and energy levels can run very low very quickly when you're injured. She needs a shot.'

Hook nodded. 'You got any ready?'

'Always. But how do we get it to her?' said Gregor.

Hook shrugged. 'Only one way.'

'What, you're gonna throw some adrenaline at her?' said Jared.

'Pretty much,' Gregor replied. 'It's in the third draw beneath table two,' he said to Hook. 'Bring them all.'

Jared watched Hook disappear and then turned on Gregor. 'How much of that stuff does she use?'
Gregor looked at Jared keenly. 'Enough to keep her and us alive.'

Stella slowed her breathing as much as she could. Her arm was shot, her body achingly tired. Deads' arms reached for her across the charnel pile. She waved them away. 'Not right now, kids. We'll play later. Mummy needs a rest.' She briefly considered laying her head down and closing her eyes, just for a few seconds. 'Don't be stupid,' she said to herself.

She couldn't decide if the noises of the deads' attempts to penetrate the hedges were getting louder or if she was getting more scared.

Fear.

It gripped her. It squeezed her insides like a fist. It was actually painful, like an extension of the agony in her shoulder. Sometimes she welcomed fear like it was the only thing that reminded her she wanted to live.

But this was too much

She had to move. That was her way, the Cynosure's way. If she was moving she couldn't be caught.

She fought the pain in her shoulder and struggled to her knees. A dead's hands were close enough to brush her hair as she swayed before it. Air moved as the tanto lashed out, slicing fingers. Stella had watched the blur of the blade as if someone else had handled the knife. 'Not good,' she said. 'Not good at all.' She fell face-first into the overgrown grass, privet branches scratching her face as she collapsed into the smell of summer, quiet days and cricket in the park.

'C'mon, c'mon!' Gregor shouted as Hook huffed and puffed back up the stairs, his arms wrapped around a dozen plastic packages.
'I'm coming as fast as I can,' the big man replied. 'Here.' He handed the plastic packs of syringes to Gregor.

'You can't throw those,' said Jared. 'Not enough weight. You'll never get it to the bushes.'

'He's right,' said Gregor.

'The bottles!' said Hook. 'Can we fit them in the bottles?'

'Might have to smash the necks open, but they should fit, yeah,' said Gregor.

'Let me,' said Jared, stopping Hook just as he was turning to run back. Jared took off, running down the stairs.

'They're on the desk in the rotunda!' Gregor shouted after him.

Jared was back in moments, breathing hard. His heart hammered in his chest. The sensation was good, natural; just a couple of days without a scare, without a reason to run or to hide, had already softened him. A racing heart meant that he was alive.

Gregor grabbed two bottles, smashed the necks against the harpoon launcher. The glass clattered to the floor along with the fuel. It pooled on the floor and the reek of diesel was strong in the air. He stuffed a plastic-wrapped syringe into each.

'From the window?' said Hook.

'You want me to do it?' said Jared.

Hook shook his head, his face determined.

Jared knew that no one else was going to help the Cynosure when Hook was around. They were too close, Jared realised. Hook accused Stella of making it about just her but Hook wanted it to be about them. Wanted Stella to feel about him the same way he felt about her. Jared wondered just how many times they must have already saved each other's lives, how many times Hook must have risked everything for her and still all she saw was the big defender from the Games. 'Okay,' he nodded. 'Bring her back.'

Hook turned to the window and threw first one and then the other bottle. 'Two more,' he said over his shoulder.

Gregor smashed the necks off two more bottles.

Through half open eyes and tall grass, Stella saw a dead fall and roll over the corpses, thudding to the ground only a couple of metres away. Her cheek was pressed against the grass and she had to look up at the creature as it started to struggle towards her, dragging itself, not bothering to get to its knees. The guttural, groaning growl from its ruined throat was like wheezing bellows filled with mucus. The sound crawled along the ground towards her, like it was alive and deliberately staying below the white noise of the deads' groans above her.

Her left arm was useless and her tanto was only lightly gripped in her right hand. Her heart was slowing, the fear not lessening, but the urgency of the terror and the panic receded to a heavy ache that covered her whole body, smothering her in dread.

Her right arm lay on the ground, pointing at the dead. She raised her head and lifted the tanto. It was so heavy. The blade wavered in front of the dead's face and would have dropped but the tip of the metal entered its mouth. Still it crawled on, its hands grasping at Stella's arm, its fingernails clawing at her skin as it inched its way towards her, its mouth sliding along the blade. Stella watched as the dead pushed itself forward, its teeth snapping on the metal, the groans turning to hideous gurgles as the tanto entered the throat and snagged. It must stop, Stella thought. But it didn't. It pushed forward. Stella felt the knife enter the top of the spine, the dead's body fell limp, its head stopped its advance just centimetres from her hand and the fingers relaxed their grip on her arm.

She let her head drop back to the grass as her grip on the tanto slackened to almost nothing.

Something grabbed the blade. Her head shot up, her grip on the blade firm again. The dead's teeth were clamped around the knife.

'Gross,' she whispered and let go of the knife as she rolled over and away from the creature's face.

Something crashed through the overgrown top of the hedge and thudded into the grass right where her head had been.

She looked up just as another object fell towards her. She rolled as quickly as she could, away from the object but towards the stack of bodies. Hands reached towards her, groping blindly, too far to reach but leaning ever closer. In moments more deads would tumble.

The objects were bottles, their necks smashed and sticking out of each of them a syringe. A familiar syringe. 'Gregor,' she gasped and dragged herself to the nearest bottle. The syringe was out and unwrapped, the clear plastic lid pulled off in her teeth to reveal the needle, in seconds. In one smooth movement she jabbed the needle into her leg and eased the adrenaline into her system.

Hook threw the fourth bottle at the hedges and turned to Gregor. 'Two more,' he said.

Jared shook his head. 'Give it a minute. You've got three right in the middle of the bushes. If she can't get to any of those then she's not getting to two more.'

'This isn't your decision,' said Hook, not even trying to take the aggression out of his voice.

'He's right,' said Gregor. 'Give it a minute.'

'A minute,' said Hook, turning back to the window. 'And then I'm going out there.'

Gregor and Jared remained silent, both realising there was no point in arguing with Hook now. Jared assessed the man's huge frame; there was little chance he could prevent him from going outside. The bulk, the muscle, the augments, would be unstoppable if Hook's mind was made up.

Jared wrinkled his nose. The smell from Hook was particularly bad.

'There!' Gregor shouted.

Jared looked away from Hook and down to see Stella just as she burst from the bush, weaving and ducking where she could and kicking and stabbing where the space was tight. Her left arm still seemed injured, the blood, some dry, some fresh, coated her arm and the clothes on her left side. She held it tightly against her chest rather than letting it swing. She made rapid if not quite straight progress, darting a metre here, two metres there, a jagged journey towards the phone box.

'She's going to make it,' Hook breathed. 'She's going to make it,' he repeated more loudly and turned to Jared. 'Be ready on that harpoon. Fire it straight through the middle of the door.'

Jared nodded, then jerked his head to the sky as a familiar sound cut through their hope.

Jet pack.

Angel.

'I'm going out there,' said Hook. He turned and ran for the stairs, grabbing a Molotov and brushing past Jared, the ex-soldier making an instinctive but half-hearted attempt to block his way.

'Wait!' Gregor called. 'It's not safe.'

But Hook was gone.

Stella ran for the phone box. Now that she was away from the bushes the deads' numbers had thinned and she was no longer bothering to take them out, just shouldering them aside. The falling bodies dominoed into each other, making her leave a wake of tottering, tumbling corpses.

Charging the last few meters to the phone box she leapt at the roof, using her right hand to steady herself as her knees slid smoothly onto the red surface. She pulled her feet up and finally turned to the window on Vic's first floor.

Her view was blocked. Unheard, the helmeted angel had approached and now it hovered between her and Vic's, the whine of its jet pack suddenly loud in her ears. 'Oh come one,' she said. 'Is that you, Vine?'

The tinted visor gave a blank response as it drifted a few metres closer.

'Vine?' Stella repeated. 'Say it ain't so, Vine.'

The angel lifted its right arm.

Stella glanced down at the ground; deads already surrounded the phone box, their thin reaching arms waving in rhythm with their groans like river reeds tossed by the passage of a boat.

Then movement behind the angel. The door of Vic's open and Hook running out, a flame, something on fire in his hand. He pulled his arm back to throw and the flame, it was a bottle, a Molotov, was launched at the angel.

Stella watched the arc of the throw; it was good. She smiled. The angel's visor remained blank.

The bottle smacked its shoulder armour just as it fired its laser, knocking the beam off target, slicing into deads on the ground to Stella's right. It bounced away, flecks of burning fuel sprinkling like fiery rain as it span and hurtled towards Stella. She saw Hook's face turn from triumph to horror as she ducked beneath the spinning bottle, wincing as the burning drops splattered her bare arms and neck. It flew on to the trees behind, smashing into a gnarled trunk and spilling its contents onto the flame.

A fireball erupted onto the tree, flames creeping and crackling across the trunk and the leaves quickly withering and dancing above the heat.

Stella looked back to the angel as it turned to her.

Jared watched the bottle, the deflected laser, saw the flames and as the angel turned on Stella he twitched the harpoon up to the angel.

'It fired,' said Gregor. 'Can't be our new friend.' He turned to Jared. 'What are you doing? You can't shoot it with a harpoon. You can't risk hitting Stella.'

Jared nodded grimly but kept the tip of the harpoon pointed at the hovering white-armoured creature.

Suddenly it moved, jerking a couple of metres to the left. It raised its arm again, but its left this time.

'What's it doing?' said Gregor. 'Shoot it. You've got a clear shot now.' He looked to Jared. 'What are you waiting for?'

'Let it do us a favour first,' said Jared. His voice was calm.

'You're taking risks you don't need to take. Shoot it!'

Even as Gregor was speaking the angel had suddenly darted forward to the fire and was spraying it with CO2, the flames quickly obscured by the thick grey gas.

Gregor's mouth dropped open and quickly shut again as he heard Hook shouting.

'Run Stella! Run!'

Jared watched as Stella measured the distance from the phone box to Vic's. She shook her head.

'Just go now! Run! You'll make it!'

Deads were already turning to stumble towards Hook's voice, towards Vic's.

'He needs to shut up,' said Gregor and then turned to Jared. 'Fire the harpoon into the phone box. That'll give Stella a way out and should shut the big ox up.'

Jared nodded, switching the harpoon to the phone box. He started to the squeeze the trigger. Then he stopped.

'What?' said Gregor. 'What is it?'

'Better idea,' said Jared, switching back to the angel. He centred the cross hair on the angel's back and waited.

'Come on.'

'Just a few seconds more.'

'Come on!'

'Wait,' said Jared. He stared at the angel's flow of gas, saw that it was lessening, slowing. It stopped.

Jared fired the harpoon.

The huge metal spear flew at the angel, catching in the middle of the back and hurling it forward, through the remains of the gas and pinning it to the blackened tree. Its arms and legs wrapped around the trunk and then fell back, lifeless.

'Shot!' Gregor yelled as Jared breathed a sigh of relief.

Stella looked up to the window and grinned at Jared who grinned back and threw in a salute. She flexed her left arm, and gingerly lifted it to salute him back and then leapt over the deads around the phone box, reaching for the harpoon's rope and catching it with both hands. Her yell of agony was clear up on the first floor of Vic's and for the deads. Heads turned to her as she swung, kicking deads aside and throwing her legs around the rope and immediately climbing towards Vic's.

Jared watched, amazed, as she covered the first few metres in just a few seconds, using her injured left arm to make sure she was out of reach of the deads as quickly as possible. The pain was etched into her face, the sweat gleaming on her forehead. Once she was clear, she slowed, returned her left arm to her chest and climbed torturously with just her right arm and her legs.

The door to Vic's slammed closed at that moment, but the damage was done; deads swarmed up the steps towards Vic's front doors.

Tash walked through the hallways of The Old Police house. The pawing of the deads at the windows was a small distraction. Hiding in a supermarket freezer with a dying brother for days on end, knowing that dozens, even hundreds of deads were on the other side of the door, had made her realise that worry was just a waste of thinking.

She sat at a table, her sparse dinner in front of her. Two empty tin cans of protein and vitamins, meat and fruit; she didn't bother to read the labels anymore. Her mobile phone waited next to the cans. She hadn't turned it on that day. Messages were guaranteed. Kyle would not want her to miss him. A grunt passed her lips as she thought of him. She had sent messages to him, tempting him.

They would meet again soon. Getting back to him was everything. Even Vine came second to Kyle.

Stella the Zombie Killer Part Seventeen

'When was the last time you went a whole day without violence?' said Jared to Hook. They leant against the harpoon, broken glass crunching beneath their boots, the stench of diesel still thick in the air.

'Couple of days ago,' Hook replied. 'We didn't go out for three days. We just did the garden, read books, cooked.'

It was dark outside, the streetlights cast an intermittent but stark white glow on the rippling mass below them. Most of the lights were still active, their solar panels still functioning three years after the death of most of the people who ever walked beneath them. The bright white dots snaked around the city, disappearing behind unlit buildings and parks, then reappearing again in the distance. From here the city was eternal. Nothing else existed but the streets and the buildings and the parks. And the deads. The noise of their movement was perpetual, natural, like the sound of the sea or the breeze in the trees or the scratching of rodents.

The two shared a bottle of red wine. Three more sat among the legs of the harpoon launcher. Jared wrinkled his nose as he looked out of the window and then held the bottle beneath his nostrils as a scented shield. 'Smells more in the city,' he said. 'There was always a smell in the country but this, this is a stink.'

'It's worse than usual.' Hook gestured to the deads. 'We don't normally have *that*.'

Jared nodded and took a swig of the wine. The alcohol was acting fast. 'I haven't had a day without violence for four months. It was back in March. Twenty of us in the camp. Nothing happened for a whole day. The scavs came back with nothing to report and no deads came near us.'

'Scavs?'

'Scavengers. Hunter-gatherer parties.'

'Not the nicest nickname.'

'Some of them used to go a bit feral. Out there, alone or in pairs, dealing with...' Jared waved the bottle at the night. 'With whatever they had to deal with. There was a split in the camp. No one really trusted them.' He took another swig and then handed the bottle to Hook, who took it and drained it, tilting his head back to let the red liquid slosh down his throat.

'She'll be alright,' said Jared.

Hook gasped as he took the bottle from his lips, the red wine visible at the corners of his mouth. He nodded. 'I know.'

'What you did was good.'

'What I did was save her,' said Hook. 'I know that and she'll realise it too.'

Jared bent to the floor and grabbed another bottle of wine. He twisted the lid. 'Imagine if all the bottles were still corked - we'd be screwed!' He laughed at his joke. He laughed hard.

'We have cork screws,' said Hook, not joining Jared in his laughter. 'And be quiet.' He nodded at the deads; Jared's barks of laughter had raised a few heads to their window and an eddy in the flow of shoulders and heads could suddenly be seen as they pushed towards the doors.

'They look like solid doors,' said Jared. 'They'll hold.' He peered out of the window onto the deads below and then looked back at Hook. 'Will they hold?'

Hook nodded. 'I wouldn't have gone out there if I didn't think they would.'

They had pulled her in, three pairs of hands trying to ease her as gently as they could back into the museum. They had laid her on the floor and then raised her again as she had groaned in pain from the broken glass. They had lifted her sweat- and blood-drenched body down to the rotunda and laid her on one of Gregor's work tables. She had passed in and out of consciousness as they had borne her like a funeral procession.

Hook's breathing was heavy with fear. He had never seen like this. Jared had tried to understand how the Cynosure could be so spent.

Gregor had reassured them. She'll be fine, he'd said.

Stella's head had lolled over their arms on her way down to the rotunda and now it was flat on the table, her whole body seemed to spread itself over the surface, making her look heavy like a dead weight. Her head rolled to one side and she looked at Hook. Their eyes met, Hook's wide with desperate hope, Stella's half-closed, narrowed by fatigue or thought or contempt. Stupid thing to do, Meathead, she had said. You never think, she had added. And then she had fallen asleep.

Silence. Except the scraping of deads' fingers and fists on the doors. The men looked over at the barred wooden barriers. They'll hold, Gregor had said. They're thicker than you, Hook, Gregor had added.

Hook had walked away from the table, upset. Gregor had focussed on Stella, so Jared had followed Hook to what turned out to be the wine store.

Jared liked wine. He hadn't had a drink in nearly three years. His hand had trembled as he reached out to the shelf.

The deads crowded below Hook and Jared. The summer night was still and heavy and their movements were gentle and soft as if a distant whisper passed among them, turning heads, tugging shoulders, making them roll together like marbles in a suede bag. Like people lost in the dark.

'We hate ourselves,' Jared slurred to Hook. 'S'obvious. We had the chance to have it all and we quite literally...' he raised his arms in the air in a mock explosion, exhaling loudly, '...blew it up. Not just blew it up, nuked it! Nuked it, for God's sake.' He took another swig from the second bottle. 'We hate ourselves.'

'Anyone ever tell you, you shouldn't drink?' said Hook.

Jared's head bounced up and down in an exaggerated nod. 'Yep. All the time. I quit for years.' He took another swig and raised his arms. 'But the nukes brought me back!' he cried dramatically. 'Humanity's hate brought me back!'

'Quiet down, Captain.' The deads had responded to Jared's outburst, the same jerking of heads towards their window, the same slosh of movement towards the doors.

'Sorry,' said Jared. His entire body suddenly sagged. 'So sorry. For everything.'

'You just need to be quieter.'

Jared sagged some more and silence descended and stretched, only to be filled by the susurrations of groans that sounded so like the murmurs of the old world, like memories of half-heard and misunderstood conversations, the words just a mumbled blur in the mind but the faces that said them still clear. As clear as blood. As clear as pain.

Jared swung his head towards Hook. 'She didn't mean it, you know. You saved her.'

'Maybe just delayed it.' Hook gestured out of the window; the glare of the white lights reflected in upturned yellow eyes.

'They'll go eventually. They're still humans, even if they're dead humans, and they'll do what humans do: give up.'

'We'll be okay. We just need thumpers,' said Hook. 'Stella could sort it in a couple of hours. One that way and one that way.' He pointed each way along Cromwell Road outside of the Victoria and Albert. 'They'd be gone in an hour.'

'No one else can take that job on?'

'I could, but... I'm slow, Cap. Too slow for a mob like that.'

Jared stumbled against the harpoon as he burped. 'Vine can do it,' he said as his stumbling feet crushed more broken glass. 'You think he'll come back?'

Hook nodded. 'They all come back for the Cynosure,' he said.

'You know,' said Jared, pointing at Hook with the bottle in his hand. 'You're either jealous as hell of her or you love her.

Hook laughed and Jared joined in. 'You love her like she's got the only kebab in the world and it's three am!' said Jared.

'Everyone loves Stella. Gregor, your son, you, Vine. This Tash'll love her when she meets her. Everyone wants a piece of her. I got to have more. I got to live with her for three years.' Hook didn't have the words for how he felt about Stella. Gardening and livestock books simply didn't give him the vocabulary. But Hook would rather be with Stella than have a hundred pigs.

'Past tense?' said Jared, pointing at the other man and narrowing his eyes as if he were some kind of inebriated investigative genius. 'You think it's over, but it's not.' Jared was shaking his head. 'It's really not.'

'Alright, I *get* to live with her. And that has to be enough.'

Jared nodded and handed Hook the bottle. The bigger man turned it upside down to his lips and drained it in three long gulps. 'She's the closest thing this world's got to a hero and I get to live with her.' He stared at Jared with the fuzzy squint of the too-drunk. Before continuing, he nodded as if he'd made up his mind about something. 'You know what she said to me once?' he slurred.

Jared shook his head as he twisted the top from another bottle of wine.

'She said to me that if I was the last man on earth, then maybe, *maybe*, she would.'

Jared nodded sympathetically. He didn't need to ask what Stella would maybe do. 'Was it just you and her here then?'

Hook shook his head mournfully. 'There's been lots of people in and out of Vic's. Three years of post-apopopliptic,' Hook stumbled over the word and waved his arms as if to drive the syllables away, 'wotnots, means you get a list of names.' He paused and looked back at the deads outside. 'Some of them might be down there.'

'Got the same list,' said Jared. He sniffed as an image of Sean slipped into his mind and then shook his head to clear it before the angels' lasers came to kill him again.

'It hits her hard.' Hook said, staring at the deads. 'When they die. She doesn't deal with it. She wants to save everyone.'

'Can't save everyone.'

Hook nodded his agreement. 'Got to love her for it though.' His sigh was long and loud. 'Made a bit of a fool of myself one time,' he confessed. 'Things were looking grim and I thought that if I didn't say it then, I never would.'

'Were you in danger? Were you about to die?'

'Yep!' Hook fell silent and stared out of the window.

'Well?' said Jared. 'What was it? Trapped? Surrounded by deads?'

Hook turned back to Jared, his face a mask of solemnity. 'The turnips were rotten.' His elbow slipped off the harpoon as he said turnips, so the word came out more as 'sturnits', but Jared understood.

'Turnips?' he said.

'Yep. Rotten. Roots was cracked. We thought that we'd never be able to grow anything! Thought it was the end. Or the beginning of the end.'

'What did you do?'

'Too much clay in the soil,' said Hook knowledgeably. 'We just got loads of bags of fertiliser from a shop and dumped it on top. Loads and loads of bags. Been fine ever since.' He burped happily as he thought of the successes in his garden.

'No,' said Jared, shaking his head so hard that he had to hold the harpoon for support. 'I mean, what did you do with Stella?'

'Made a fool of myself, Cap. Laid it on the line. Spilled my guts as surely as if she'd knifed me. Which she did. Of at least it felt like it. "Not if you were the last man on Earth!" she said. I said to her, C'mon, if I was really the last, the very, *very* last, you would. "No!" she said. You would, I said. Anyway, she finally says to me, "Maybe." *Maybe!*'

'That's awful,' said Jared. 'That's really awful.'

Hook nodded, reaching for and then cuddling the bottle of wine.

'That's really awful. I mean *really* awful. How do you get over something like that? And you've got to see her every day! How do you cope with seeing her every day?'

Hook turned back to the window and the groaning stinking deads and the eternal city of lights. 'Turnips,' he said, nodding sagely. 'Nothing picks you up like a good turnip.'

Tash and Vine ate their meal in the dark, just a single lit candle so that they could see each other. The angel had stayed out as long as he could, drinking the last of the rays of the sunshine.

'It's good,' he said, between massive mouthfuls.

Tash liked to watch him eat. He could like a horse, her mum would have said. She used to say it about her brother, about Arek. He could eat like a horse and swim like a fish. He could have swum in the Olympics, Mum had always said.

She nodded at Vine, smiling. 'Good,' she said. 'Plenty more where that came from. You want extras?'

Vine nodded gratefully, smiling like a teenage boy.

It was chicken curry. Tinned of course, and there was no rice. But there was meat and a spicy taste and the smell took them back in time. Vine spooned up every drop she gave him, the fleshy half of his face bright red in the candle's flickering light.

'We go tomorrow,' said Tash, her eyes gleaming as they reflected the flame. 'And the Cynosure will fight for us.'

Stella the Zombie Killer Part Eighteen

Stella stared at the blue and green chandelier suspended above the desk in the rotunda. She shifted on Gregor's work table. There was a small pillow but nothing else. Even so, her eyes lids were heavy, drooping as sleep tugged on them with heavy fingers, but she didn't want to sleep. Not yet. The clawed fingers of deads still groped at her ankles as she swung on the rope, the rough hemp of the rope still scoured the skin on her palms, the dizziness was still swirling in her head, making her feel sick as if she were drunk and the memory of the pain in her shoulder was something solid in her mind, as if someone had opened her skull and held a light bulb to the back of her brain.

'Don't fight it,' said Gregor. 'Sleep. I can work on you in the morning.'

'Did anyone ever tell you have a wonderful way with words?' Stella muttered.

'No,' said Gregor. He was bending over her, shining a light into one of her eyes. He had already cleaned and bandaged her arm, the stark white of the dressing brilliant against her black vest and filthy flesh, but the rest would have to wait until she had rested.

'Not surprised,' she said, trying to smile but looking like she had forgotten how.

Gregor's head bobbed in and out of Stella's vision. The chandelier gave him a blue-green halo.

'You're an angel,' said Stella. Her voice was woozy. Gregor had injected her with morphine and she felt nothing but sickness and memories.

Gregor grunted. 'Could do with one of those. Your new friend coming back?'

'Gonna bring a friend. Gonna fly.' Stella giggled. 'Can't get in the front door. He'll have to land in the garden. Hook will be mad. Meathead mad. Jealous mad. Runner-bean mad. Can you get garden rage? Seems like you should. Hook the slug killer!'

'Sleep now,' said Gregor, ignoring her rants. 'It's the best rest you can get.'

'Don't like the view,' said Stella, her voice sulky. 'Don't like the view,' she repeated.

'You want some help to sleep?'

Stella nodded dopily. Gregor grabbed a syringe from a cupboard beneath the desk. 'Just the one shot,' he said to her gently. 'Just to help you sleep.' He grabbed cotton wool and tipped a bottle of antiseptic up into it. Pulling her arm gently towards him, he turned it over to reveal the inside of her elbow. She was still streaked with sweat and blood and dirt. He dabbed at her skin with the cotton wool, revealing the tanned flesh beneath. Her muscles were small but dense, like rocks just below the surface of a running river. 'It'll only hurt for a second,' he said, hushing her as she groaned a little. He slid the needle into her vein and pressed the liquid into her blood stream.

Immediately her eyes drifted closed. 'Take a little nap now,' she mumbled. 'Do the chickens tomorrow.'

'Chickens can wait,' Gregor agreed.

All night long the deads pushed against the solid wooden doors. Gregor had had one last check after helping Stella to fall asleep. There was no strain on the bars, the deads' scraping and tapping no more hurtful to the wood than rain. No one bothered to watch the doors as all through the Victoria and Albert the survivors slept, fitfully, through the bland noise and the darker hours.

Hook snored loudly. Jared, his head spinning after he had vomited into the water reclamation unit, had rolled off the cafeteria benches and now cuddled his coat on the floor. Gregor had stared at the ceiling for a long time, memories of the deads he had faced and Stella's wounds racing through his mind.

Across the city, not far, walk-able in a time before, an angel slept peacefully in a once-grand house in a once-grand park.

Tash and Vine never slept together. Tash wasn't even sure if Vine could still do what it was that people did when they shared a bed. She would, if he wanted to. She was lonely and he was a good looking man, a decent man. She'd met few enough of those in the past three years. Even before the crash she'd met nothing but users and abusers. Only her brother had saved her faith in men. The one decent man she knew, made all the others seem like they could be saved. Vine reminded her of her brother.

She smiled as she stared at the ceiling, sleep as allusive as kind men. The thought of meeting the Cynosure was too much. All those times Tash had helped her brother with the Lynxes, all those players and none of them like the Cynosure. The Killer was someone worth working on. But that wasn't the job.

She rolled over and screwed her eyes tight. Eventually sleep came.

'Someone's been sick in the water rec,' said Gregor to Hook and Jared. They were both seated at the desk in the rotunda. Both nursed their heads.

Stella's table was empty; Gregor had helped her to her sparse bed in the former gift shop.

Hook groaned. 'Wasn't me. Don't think it was me.' He shrugged. 'Could've been me.'

'It was me,' said Jared, stirring from his torpor. 'I'm really sorry, Gregor. I'll clean it up.' His thoughts had been on the wine rack in the kitchens.

'No use now,' said Gregor. 'It's sucked most of it up. We'll just have to hold our noses when we drink.'

Hook twisted his face in disgust. 'Nice one, Cap!'

'Doesn't really matter,' said Gregor to Hook, 'you're drinking everyone's urine, remember?' He turned back on Jared. 'But the lumps cause a problem.'

'Sorry,' Jared repeated.

Hook turned to Gregor. 'She okay?' he said, nodding his head towards the gift shop.

'She'll be okay. Cuts and bruises for the most part. Suspected fracture in her left humerus.' Gregor saw the blank looks and explained: 'The bone in her upper arm.'

The other two men nodded. 'Won't that affect her wings?' said Hook.

Gregor shrugged. 'They haven't worked in years.'

'Wings?' said Jared.

'Shunters,' said Hook. 'All the strikers had them.'

Gregor nodded. 'They help them get past the defence in the games. An augment solidifies the flesh around the humerus and expands the bone, makes a battering ram out of the upper arm and shoulder. It's how someone like Stella could shunt someone like Hook aside as if they weren't there.'

Jared was nodding his head, remembering. 'Don't try this at home,' he said. 'It's what my son used to say. He used to shout it, like it was a chant or something.'

'It was,' said Hook. 'It was part of the magic of the games. They were always open about the augments but when someone could use them as effectively as Stella it was magic. No one could do what she did. No one called her shunters *shunters*. She had wings because she flew at her opponents. She did things with augments that other gamers couldn't do let alone normal people.' Hook smiled at the memory. 'So don't try it at home.'

Jared was nodding again. 'She's like a snow plough.'

'She was,' Gregor agreed. 'But that augment hasn't worked in a long while.'

'What about the angel pieces?' said Jared. 'There must be something we can do with them? It's similar tech isn't it?'

Hook shrugged. 'Not my department.' He looked at Gregor.

'It might be possible,' he said. 'But I don't know how. Her arm is broken, so that's the first thing we fix. As for the augments,' he shrugged. 'She's got this far without them.'

Jared stared at Gregor through the fog of his hangover. He was thinking of the wine store, knowing that he could slip away, sort out his head. He shook himself. 'A fitter Cynosure would be best for all of us,' he said, keeping his voice steady. 'It makes sense to try.'

'It's a risk. A big risk. I get it wrong and we've got a one-armed Cynosure.'

Hook raised his hands. 'Let's slow down on this, yeah? I'm with Gregor; Stella's done a pretty stellar job so far. No point risking anything.'

'It'd be nice to be asked,' said a voice behind them. Stella glared at each of them in turn as she walked steadily towards the desk. Her left arm was held securely in a sling. 'Planning my future, boys?'

'It wasn't like that, Stella,' said Hook.

Stella ignored him and bore down on Jared. 'You're new, Mr Jenks, so I'll let you in on a special secret.' She leaned close to him, her eyes were dark, sunk into her pale face. Jared leaned towards her, the bruise on his jaw was just starting to bloom. 'I'm not a tool,' she said quietly. 'I'm not a key piece in your strategies. I'm not playing a game. I'm not the Cynosure. But most of all, I'm not a damned snow plough.'

Jared nodded his head nervously. 'Of course not,' he stammered. 'I just meant...' He gave up, knowing that Stella knew exactly what he had meant.

Stella turned on Gregor. 'Well?' she said. 'What did you want to ask me?'

Gregor nodded nervously. 'Your arm's broken, Stella. That and there's so many cuts and bruises on you I can't assess the damage clearly. You're looking at a lot of down time. At least two weeks, maybe a month. Jared's got a point; if I'm fixing your arm anyway, we could maybe scavenge something from the angels and sort out your wings.'

'Can you do it?' she said to Gregor. 'You didn't sound too confident.'

'They haven't worked in so long,' he replied. 'I just can't be certain.'

Stella nodded. 'Then we set the bone and wait it out. There's enough risk already.'

'What did we lug this stuff back for?' said Hook, waving an arm at the angel parts on the tables. 'We should make some use of it.'

'And we will,' said Stella. 'But we'll do it sensibly, not stupidly. No need to run outside and throw fire bombs.'

Hook stared at Stella for a moment. 'No need to thank me, boss,' he said.

'No need at all,' she replied coolly. 'There are a couple of thousand thank yous outside the front door.'

'We'll get it sorted. Vine can set a couple of thumpers once he gets here. They'll be gone before you can say wow-Hook-you-saved-my-life.'

Stella ignored him and turned back to Gregor. 'This thing's giving me trouble,' she said indicated her left arm.

'Painful?' said Gregor. Stella nodded. 'I'll give you something then we can set it. I've no plaster but a splint will do fine.'

Hook threw one last glare at Stella and then turned and left.

Jared watched him go. 'He maybe acted a little rashly,' he said to Stella, 'but he did save your life. That angel had you.'

Stella glared at Jared. 'That angel had nothing.' Her stare hardened, daring him to speak again.

Jared nodded and lowered his eyes.

Hook tended his garden. He tied the beans that had fallen since the day before. He trimmed, he turned, he picked, his fingers green and brown, the nails filthy.

'Can I help?' said Jared.

'Can you stay on your feet?' Hook replied. 'I'm sorry,' he said as Jared's face fell. 'That was out of order. You can grab the eggs from the chicken run and clean out the rabbits. We'll clean the chickens out together tomorrow. Unless you've done it before?'

Jared nodded, grateful for the distraction and then shook his head. 'I haven't cleaned out chickens before but I'll manage some eggs and rabbits.' He grabbed a basket and went for the eggs first, gingerly moving the chickens out of the way. Hook laughed at him for his caution and pretty soon he was moving around the run with more confidence and a dozen eggs sat in his basket. 'Omelettes for dinner and tea,' he said, smiling.

His smile faded as he heard the jet pack.

Hook heard it too and the two men moved to the edge of the garden to shelter in the shadows of the museum. He held up his hand to quiet Jared and the two men waited in silence.

The sound circled the museum, the loud whine of the engine strained as if it were hovering or over-worked. And then two figures drifted into view, stark against the blue sky, from behind the roofs; an angel and someone else, carried, red-shoed feet dangling. As they descended to the garden Hook and Jared could see that it was Vine and a woman. She wore blue jeans, a clean white t-shirt and red Converse trainers. She carried two plastic bags and a large rucksack was strapped across her chest. Vine held the straps as a harness. The woman smiled at them, while Vine focussed on the landing, setting her down gently among a row of broccoli.

Hook tutted as the exhaust from the jet pack battered his plants.

Tash picked her way through the crop, carefully avoiding damaging anything. She kept glancing up from her careful steps to Hook and Jared and smiling.

Vine shut off his jet pack, the wheezing wind down sputtering and hissing, and followed more awkwardly but no less carefully, his massive, armoured bulk strange in the green space.

Hook ignored the angel and appraised Tash quickly. She was a good-looking woman, younger than he'd expected, younger than Stella, but healthy, or as healthy as anyone three years in. Her teeth and clothes were clean, her pale hair shined, she walked carefully but confidently. Hook liked her immediately.

'Welcome,' he said.

'Hi,' she said as she finally moved close enough to drop her bags and reach out a hand. Her smile was wide, her teeth shining white. 'I'm Tash. Thanks so much for letting us come. It's crazy out there.'

Stella the Zombie Killer Part Nineteen

Ben, his heavy-lidded eyes hooded and dark, watched the Victoria and Albert Museum from the cover of the trees across the road. He was a scrawny man, thin and wasted, but not skeletal. Muscles, taut and ready, strained against his skin, like scarabs trying to escape a cadaver. There was a rifle slung across his back. It was a bulky thing, made from hard white plastics and silver metals. It was not like the rifles from before the Message. This was new tech. This was something from the People.

The watcher wrinkled his nose; the faint whiff of scorched wood still wafted from the crucified angel affixed to the tree trunk just a few metres away from him. The smell only occasionally rose above the stench of decay and Ben made regular sweeps of an aftershave bottle beneath his nose.

The apocalypse had suited him. He had more freedoms, more powers, more of everything. He was respected in this world. But the smell. The smell drove him crazy.

The sound of a jetpack jerked his head to the sky. There they were. Tash and her pet angel. The big guy carried her, the whine of his engines the telltale sound of desperation.

'You can't hide forever,' he said to the flying pair. He took a mobile from his pocket, pointed it at the two of them and took a picture just before they disappeared behind the buildings of the V and A. He scrolled through a short list of contacts until the name Kyle appeared on the screen. His thumb dabbed on the name, opening the message screen. He attached the photo and wrote the message: *found her*

He pressed send.

'Hi,' said Tash to Gregor. Her voice was light and friendly, echoing slightly to the high glass ceiling. 'Gregor, right? Chief bio-mech of the Mariners?'

The old bio-mech was alone in the rotunda. He grunted a reply.

Tash still held the bulging carrier bags and Vine loomed behind her, carrying her rucksack. Hook walked with her, smiling at her whenever he could and Jared trailed after them, watching and listening.

'Wow,' said Tash as she approached the desk and Gregor's work stations. Her eyes were wide with wonder. 'Vine said you had some cool stuff but this is unbelievable.' She placed the carrier bags next to the desk with a heave of clinking noises, and stepped through the gap into Gregor's work area. The man frowned his annoyance at her but she either ignored him or was just too excited to notice. 'Is that an infra-red retro-reflective camera?'

Gregor nodded, the scowl still firmly on his face.

'2D or 3D?' Tash asked.

'Both,' said Gregor.

'Wow! And is that a Kistler Piezoelectric 3D Force Platform?'

Gregor nodded, his frown slipping as Tash's enthusiasm began to worm into him. 'You worked with the Lynxes?'

'Uh-huh,' Tash nodded and then dashed to more of Gregor's exotic pieces of equipment. 'A 3D accelerometer? Isokinetiv Dynamometer with integrated PC? Force distribution instrumentation for measuring impact? Applied VR simulator?'

All the questions were rushed in an excited gabble and Gregor nodded to every one of them, his frown turning closer and closer to a smile with every affirmative.

'And of course a big pile of laptops!' She patted the stack of portable computers. 'And a running machine. Wow, it's huge! I bet Vine could have a jog on that beast.'

'Well, Hook's about the biggest I'd risk,' said Gregor.

'Of course,' said Tash, smiling widely. 'I'm only teasing.' She turned to Hook. 'I thought I recognised you. You're Hook of the Falcons. Have you still got the move?'

Hook smiled like a school boy and shot out his right arm in hooking motion. 'Hook 'em in,' he said happily.

Tash giggled at the motion and then looked around the rest of the party. 'Where is she?' she said, her voice dropping to a loud whisper. 'Where's the Cynosure?'

'Resting,' said Gregor.

'Rough night?' said Tash.

'You could say that.' Stella's voice reached from behind the group. 'More of a rough few days, but you'd already know that, what with you listening in with your big friend.'

Tash's eyes widened as Stella moved into view. She was as star struck as all the others who met Stella. The sight of the Cynosure was a post-apocalyptic miracle, as unbelievable as the idea of the dead walking had been just three years ago. 'I...' she paused, not knowing what to say and instead just pointed at Stella' arm.

Stella looked down at the sling and shrugged. 'Could've been worse.'

'How are your shunters?' said Tash. 'Must have been a big bang to get through them.'

Gregor coughed with embarrassment and raised one hand to scratch the back of his head. 'Stella's erm, wings, erm, don't exactly work anymore,' he said. His voice was awkward and his face was red.

'Really?' said Tash. She looked at Stella. The Killer's eyes were hard and penetrating. 'How long for?'

'Not really any of your business,' Stella replied. She looked Tash up and down and then grunted at her. 'Wrists and ankles.'

'What?' said Tash.

'Wrists and ankles,' said Stella. 'I need to see your wrists and ankles.'

'C'mon, Stella,' said Hook. 'You can see her wrists are clear from here, and her ankles wouldn't fit into those fine new shoes if they were bitten or torn up.' He turned to Tash. 'Nice outfit, by the way.'

Tash blushed and smiled as she received the compliment. 'Thank you,' she said.

'Not very practical,' Stella pointed out.

'If you can't get some new clothes when you visit London, when can you?' said Hook, smiling broadly at Tash.

'Ankles,' said Stella.

Tash raised one foot to the desk and peeled the hem of her tight jeans up and away from her clean ankle.

Stella studied it before nodding and gesturing for Tash to do the same with the other.

Tash paused, looking around the group as if for support.

Hook and Gregor shrugged and waited. Jared narrowed his eyes. Vine simply nodded.

Tash raised her foot and her jeans. The group leant forward to inspect the pale flesh. There were marks around her ankle; ugly red scars that looped the double domes of her ankle bones.

'What's that?' said Stella

'Nothing,' Tash replied. 'Just a memento.'

'You've been treated badly?' Hook asked. His voice was filled with concern, so much so that Stella glanced at him.

Tash just shrugged and smiled. 'There's been worse than me since the crash.'

'That doesn't matter; they didn't feel it,' said Jared. Everyone looked at him, surprised. It was the first time he had spoken since Tash and Vine had arrived. The soldier looked to Tash with some sympathy and then shrugged and fell back into silence.

Tash just nodded an agreement. 'I just meant it could've been worse.'

'What happened?' said Hook.

'Men,' Tash replied. 'Not nice men.'

Stella's eyes narrowed as she measured Tash. The younger woman was pretty, her smile easy, her teeth white, her short blonde hair shining in the rotunda's squares of sunlight. Her new clothes made her look new somehow, as if she had been created right before she entered Vic's. 'I know you,' she said, her tone accusing.

'I think I'd remember meeting the Cynosure,' said Tash. She laughed.

Stella heard the force in the laugh, could feel it pushed out of the woman's mouth. 'I've seen you before,' she said.

Tash shook her head. 'Impossible.'

'The phone,' said Stella. 'Gregor, where's the phone?'

Gregor turned to one of his work desks; the phone was still plugged into one of his laptops. He unhooked it and threw it to Stella.

Tash's eyes widened as she watched the phone arc through the air towards Stella. She threw a glance at Vine but he either didn't notice or was deliberately ignoring her.

Stella snatched the phone with her good hand and thumbed it open. She held the phone out to Tash, the screen saver with the man and the woman clearly visible. 'Is that you?'

Tash stepped forward nervously. She looked at the image. She nodded.

The woman in the picture had long blonde hair but it was obviously Tash.

'Where did you find it?' said Tash.

'In a hotel not too far from here,' said Stella. 'Over in Earl's Court. The battery was still nearly full, so it'd been dropped recently. Who's the man?'

'One of the not very nice men,' said Tash simply. She held Stella's stare, her own eyes shining with sudden tears. 'He obviously hasn't forgotten me.'

'How long since you've seen him?' said Jared.

Tash looked his way, grateful to be released from Stella's penetrating stare. 'More than a year. He's the reason I left London.'

'Did you know about this?' said Stella to Vine.

Vine shrugged. 'Some of it.'

'And you didn't think it would be a good idea to warn us that your friend comes with baggage?' said Stella. Her voice was rising, her anger growing.

Vine shrugged again, infuriating Stella further. 'It's been three years of chaos and death,' he said. 'Who doesn't have baggage?'

'Not everyone has crazy ankle-chaining baggage!' Stella snapped.

'So what are saying, Stella?' said Hook. 'We save who we can as long as it's easy?'

Stella turned on Hook but stopped herself from speaking. She turned back to Tash who withered a little under her gaze. 'Can we expect a visit from this man?'

'I honestly don't know,' said Tash, a tear leaking from her left eye and rolling down her cheek. 'Kyle had lots of girls. I was no one special.' She hung her head, her shame suddenly obvious.

Hook and Vine stepped forward, but Stella was there first, her face still serious but softened towards the younger woman. She held Tash's shoulders. 'Well,' she said. 'You're safe now.'

Tash looked up and beamed. 'Thank you,' she said as she wiped the tears from her cheeks and scrubbed at her eyes. Her voice was respectful, humble, almost reverent. 'And maybe I can help you,' she added, pointing at Stella's arm. 'With this equipment, it would be easy.' Suddenly, her hand flew to her mouth and she turned to Gregor. 'I'm sorry,' she said. 'I didn't mean to...'

Gregor held up a hand. 'It's fine,' he said, trying to sound casual. But his cheeks blazed. 'If you can help, we should get started as soon as possible.'

'Brilliant,' Tash replied before sniffing away the last of her tears. 'I've brought a few bits and bobs as well.' She hefted the carrier bags and then turned to the angel. 'Vine? Do you mind taking the rucksack to wherever we can get set up while I stay with Gregor?'

'Not a problem,' Vine replied.

'Come on then, toaster,' said Hook. 'We can set you up in the old Room to Damascus. We dragged a few sofas in there years ago. It's pretty comfy.' The two men lumbered away, Hook was six inches shorter than the angel but still an imposing figure.

'Pair of meat heads,' said Stella.

Jared grunted a laugh. 'I'll go with them,' he said. 'I could do with moving out of the cafeteria.'

'See you later, Captain Jenks,' said Stella. She turned back to Tash. Stella was all business again, the previous warmth gone. 'Just what is it that you think you can do?'

Tash's smile never slipped even though Stella's tone was less than friendly. 'With the 3D force platform and the retro-reflective camera we can start running sims immediately.' Her voice was muffled as she bent to her bags. 'I've got a special set of cameras that I've been dying to use.' She hauled one bulky black plastic box after the other onto the desk until there were four head-sized ugly-looking plastic devices sitting on the wooden top.

'Are they...?' Gregor began and then paused, not daring to voice his question in case it wasn't what he hoped it was. Instead, he just let his mouth fall open in amazement.

'What?' said Stella, eyeing the unimpressive boxes.

'ARaMIS digital imagers,' said Tash. Stella thought that she said it smugly, but seeing the look on Gregor's face made her realise that this was something to be smug about in bio-mech circles.

'And?' she said. 'What's a musketeer got to with anything?'

Gregor and Tash looked to each other and smirked as if Stella was the thick kid in a maths classroom full of number geeks

Gregor saw Stella's thunderous face and snapped his mouth shut. 'This is NASA tech,' he explained. 'Automation, Robotics and Machine Intelligence Systems. It's used for measuring stress on spacecraft. With these we could make calculations with parameters stringent enough to fix your augments.'

'Which ones?' said Stella.

Gregor let out a gasp. 'All of them,' he said.

'How many need work?' said Tash.

Gregor and Stella swapped a look that made Tash raise her eyebrows. 'All of them,' Gregor repeated.

Hook and Jared tried not to laugh as they watched Vine try to set up the Room for Damascus. The cyborg's attempt at these few domestic tasks were not far off a total failure as his armoured bulk knocked and caught and swiped the things that he was trying to arrange. 'I think I'll leave it to Tash,' he eventually said. The other two burst out laughing.

'I can just see you in a pinnie,' said Hook.

Vine grunted a deep warning rumble which Hook ignored.

'You could have a robot in its underwear on the front,' said Hook. Jared smirked.

Vine ignored him. 'Where do I sleep?' he said.

'Oh,' said Hook. 'Are you and Tash not...?'

'No,' Vine replied. 'We're not.'

Hook nodded. 'Have you ever...?'

'No,' Vine replied. 'We have not.'

Hook was silent for a moment, an unusual look of thoughtfulness on his face. 'Can you... erm...?' Hook nodded at his own groin.

'What?' said Vine.

'You know,' said Hook, nodding at his own groin again.

'Did you want me to do something with that?' Vine said, gesturing at Hook's groin.

All three men laughed.

'C'mon,' said Hook. 'We'll set you up next door in Musical Wonders of India.'

They followed Vine through to the next room, dumped his stuff and turned to head back to the rotunda.

'Fancy a trip out, Robby?' said Hook to Vine.

Vine sighed in return. 'I don't even get that one,' he said, his voice deadpan.

'Robby the Robot,' said Jared. 'From 'The Forbidden Planet'. It was a movie.'

Vine nodded but didn't smile. 'What do you need?' he said to Hook.

'The deads away from our doors. A man of your jetpack talents could fly out with a couple of thumpers and have them cleared in a couple of hours,' said Hook.

'Isn't the range limited on those things?' said Jared.

Hook shrugged. 'About six of seven hundred metres, I think. Should give us a about a mile.'

'That's risky,' said Jared. 'What with Gregor's thumper just round the corner yesterday, we could be attracting a lot of angels to the area around Vic's. The one that went for Stella yesterday must have been from Gregor's thumper.'

'It's a risk we'll have to take, Cap. We can't stay stuck in here forever.'

'There must be back doors,' said Jared.

'We barricaded them,' said Hook. 'Years ago. We decided it was easier just having one way in and one way out.'

'You must have some kind of escape plan,' said Vine.

'We've got the harpoons. We can set up a rope bridge at the front, back and sides, but we'd rather not use that up for the sake of a few deads,' said Hook.

'There are more than a few,' Vine warned. 'When I flew over to get here, the whole museum was surrounded. The deads have nowhere else to go.'

'Then let's give them a sense of purpose,' said Hook.

'Then we open one of the back doors,' said Vine.

Hook shrugged. 'I suppose it's not a problem.'

'I'll see you guys later,' said Jared. 'I need a new room, so I'll go check a few out.' The other two nodded at him. 'I'll not be long I shouldn't think,' he continued. 'Just half an hour so.'

'Okay, Cap,' said Hook. 'No worries.'

Jared started to speak again, stopped himself and nodded to the other men. He turned away from them and headed for the wine store.

Stella the Zombie Killer Part Twenty

Ben only ever wanted respect. Kyle's organisation was the new world order and Ben was proud of his role in it. His autonomy showed trust and respect. Respect was important to Ben. He needed it, thrived off it, even if he thought he wasn't getting it. Especially if he thought he wasn't getting it. In the old world he had always been in trouble about one thing or another. But Kyle respected him. He knew it. *Keep watch* the message from Kyle had read. *I'll send some spy stuff for you.* Kyle always made sure that Ben was well-equipped. He got to work alone and he got the best toys to go with it. Respect.

'I can't go today,' said Vine to Hook. They were in the rotunda, eating a dinner and talking about placing the thumpers. Stella, Tash and Gregor were also present. 'If I keep flying, I'll eventually draw attention to us. We could have angels flying into the garden.'

'We need these deads clearing,' said Hook. 'There's no guarantee that the doors are going to hold.'

'Another day won't hurt,' said Stella. 'Besides, we've been pretty quiet; the deads might do a bit of scraping but they're not getting through.'

Silence fell around the desk and, as if to illustrate Stella's point, the faint noise of scraping and pawing against the solid wooden doors could be heard.

Stella nodded. 'We could even leave it a week before you fly again. We're well-stocked and there's plenty that needs doing around the place.' She looked to Hook. 'Chickens need cleaning out.' She smiled as she said it and Hook returned the grin eagerly.

'A job for Captain Jenks, I think,' he said.

Stella nodded. 'Where is Jared?' she said.

'He was checking out the rooms,' said Vine. 'Has he been sleeping in the cafeteria? Anyway, he needs somewhere new, he says.'

'We can get to work this afternoon,' said Gregor to Stella. 'Tash and me already started creating sims for the work on your arm. We should have an idea of where we're going with it by tomorrow. This afternoon, as long as Tash doesn't mind, I can sort out your ocular implants.'

'No problem,' said Tash. 'I can run the sims and start checking Vine over as well. We haven't had the luxury of all this equipment; he needs a thorough check-up.'

'I am sitting here, you know,' said Vine.

'Sorry,' said Tash, smiling at her friend. 'I get talking shop and I forget.'

'Okay,' Stella agreed. 'Start on me and Vine this afternoon. The sooner we're up and running again, the sooner the deads are cleared.'

Hook shuddered. 'Pleased it's you, not me, boss. Can't stand the thought of messing about with eyes.'

Ben aimed his rifle at the nearest zombie and fired. The beam was set to its lowest power level but it was more than enough to drop the creature like a bag of rags as a neat hole was instantly drilled through its head.

He was making his way to the Ismaili Centre, having decided to set up his base there. It would give him an excellent view of the museum and keep the zombies at bay. They were easy to deal with but tiresome in numbers and constancy.

Ben shot two more, quick and silent beams of energy lancing from his rifle, killing so quickly that both simply fell to their knees and stayed there as if in supplication to their killer. Ben watched as their heads slumped forward, the motion enough to topple their bodies to the ground.

He liked to kill the zombies. Their previous lives opened up to him as he took aim. The last two had both been clothed in decaying grey suits. One still had a tie around its neck. They had left their office at lunch time, looking for a bite to eat and perhaps a drink. Nothing too strong; too much work to do that afternoon. And the kids would need some time in the evening. Ben imagined the children waiting for their dads to come home. Waiting to watch the People make their first landing on Earth. Watching the missiles and turning to their mums: 'Will Daddy be watching?' And Mum would tell them that Daddy was already dead but that they shouldn't be too sad as they would also be dead soon.

Ben spat on the nearest corpse. He'd had it coming. They all had.

He moved away, back into the line of trees to skirt around behind the Ismaili Centre so as not to draw the zombies away from the museum. He wouldn't want Tash and her friend to miss the fun of clearing their new hideout.

'So,' said Tash as she focused on the simulators running on the computer monitor. The images showed various body parts impacting with various objects. Data scrolled across the screen, Tash's eyes darting this way and that to monitor the results. 'How have you got by with so many of your augments not working?'

Stella shrugged as Gregor prised her eye out.

'Stay still,' the old man grunted.

'I'd rather clean the chickens,' said Hook, staring with fascination at Stella's empty eye socket.

'What about Jared?' said Stella.

Hook shrugged. 'Dunno.'

'Well, don't sit there and stare. Go sort the garden,' Stella commanded.

'Sir!' said Hook, slamming his heels together and saluting. He turned and headed away from the rotunda to his garden.

'Well?' said Tash. 'Any extra information would help. Maybe your body has kept some of the augments.'

'Stims and painkillers,' said Stella. She said it matter-of-factly, as if it didn't matter.

Tash turned away from the screen to stare at Stella. 'For three years?'

'No,' said Gregor. 'Some failed more quickly than others. Some still have much of their original function. Legs are in pretty good shape, and arms, except for the shunters, have still given Stella extra strength. At least the arms used to be okay,' he added, nodding his head at the bandaging on Stella's arm.

'The torso?' said Tash.

'Not functioned correctly for over a year,' said Gregor.

'So the compensators and shock absorbers haven't been working?' said Tash, her voice incredulous.

'Hence the pain killers,' said Stella.

Tash stared from one to the other. 'That's not safe.'

'Probably not,' Gregor agreed.

'We've discussed it,' said Stella. 'We haven't had much choice if we want to move about the city.'

'Well, I can help you with it all,' said Tash. She smiled as if she were a doctor on a mission of mercy. She glanced at Gregor. 'We'll have you fully fit in a week. At least,' she added, 'the augments will be fine. Your arm may take a little longer.'

Stella glanced to Gregor, who nodded his agreement. 'That'd be nice,' she said. 'I think I could do with a rest.' Stella's voice was suddenly tired, more tired than Gregor had ever heard it.

'I have one thing to ask in return,' said Tash.

Gregor and Stella both looked to her in surprise. 'I didn't know we were bargaining,' said Stella.

Tash smiled. 'It's not for me. It's for Vine.' She spread her arms to include all of Gregor's equipment. 'With all this I can help him.'

'To do what?' said Stella.

'To have it all,' said Tash. 'To be able to access all his systems.'

'Including his weapons?' said Stella.

Tash nodded.

'We'll have to talk about that,' said the Cynosure.

Ben didn't have to wait long for the equipment. Kyle had started using bicycles almost straight away. Vehicles, especially petrol or diesel engines, made too much noise and attracted zombies on every journey.

The solar cars and vans weren't always reliable, especially in the beginning when the clouds made their permanent night. Bicycles were fast and quiet and with panniers could move lighter equipment about the city without attracting attention.

Two of Kyle's workers had brought it, Craig and Steph. Ben didn't like Craig. The other man didn't show much respect. Steph was okay, more than okay. Ben liked the summer because the women wore shorts. The shorts made up for the smell of the city.

They had helped him drag the surveillance equipment inside and then left him to set it up, promising daily returns with supplies.

Ben never thanked them, especially Craig. Craig could go hang for all Ben cared. But he looked forward to seeing Steph every day.

He had thermal imaging cameras to monitor the museum and motion alarms pointed at the doors. He would be able to take breaks and sleep and still know if they left the place.

The purple and red images of people walking in and out of the rooms at the front of the museum criss-crossed the screen of his monitor like multi-coloured pools of oil sliding across water. Within an hour he knew there were at least four people in the museum. One of them was obviously the living angel while another was male and it looked like Tash had another woman in there with her.

He sent a text to Kyle requesting a listening device. The reply was quick. *No problem.*

'We need to think about this,' said Hook. He was with Gregor and Stella in the cafeteria. A few of Jared's effects, a blanket, his old shoes, were scattered on the floor.

'He could be useful,' said Gregor. 'He'd clear those deads out there in no time.'

'He could clear us out as well,' said Hook.

'The rest of us have tried a little harder to get along with him,' said Stella to Hook, her tone admonishing.

Hook held his hands apart in appeasement. 'Hey, I like the guy. Always have. I'm just saying that's a lot of power for one man.'

'We need Jared's input on this,' said Gregor. 'He used to work in angel control. Maybe we can activate his weapons and still have some kind of fail safe.'

'Where is he?' said Stella.

At that moment the door to the cafeteria slowly opened and Jared entered. A look of surprise passed across his face as he saw the other three. Surprise and something else.

Stella stared hard at the former captain. Even though she felt exhausted, she saw more clearly. Her bionic eye was fully operational, and she had spent a pleasurable half hour scrolling through her long-missed functions. Zooming and scanning and shutting herself in the cloakroom to test the night vision. Plus a new function. 'I hear I need to thank you for my new targetter,' she said in as friendly a voice as she could.

Jared just nodded. 'No problem,' he mumbled

Now Stella looked closely at Jared's face and she didn't like what she saw. 'You okay, Mr Jenks?'

'I'm fine,' Jared replied more loudly. He spoke slowly, carefully forming each word. He crossed the distance between them, carefully avoiding chairs and tables. 'How are you?' he said as he approached the table.

Stella rubbed her eyes. 'Tired,' she said, 'and not ready for anymore mysteries. Where have you been?'

Jared sat heavily on the empty chair at their table. 'Looking for a room. There's one at the back, some old shoes and comfy seats. Think I'll set up there.'

'That's a long way from the rest of us, Cap,' said Hook. He was staring at him, thoughtfully. 'Do we smell?'

Stella glanced at Hook; the big man always smelled.

'No, of course not.' Jared said this more hurriedly, not taking such care over the way he said the words. He slurred.

'You're drunk,' said Gregor.

Jared shook his head. 'No, not at all.'

Hook wrinkled his nose. 'I can smell it. How can you after last night? My stomach's been like a tumble drier all day.'

'I think you need to stay close by, Jared,' said Stella. Her voice was soft with tiredness and compassion. 'You can't be on your own, not like this.'

Jared hung his head. 'I can't…' he stopped. 'I just can't.'

'You can,' said Stella. She reached over to him, her hand flat on the table. Hook looked at her hand and then looked away. 'We'll help,' she said.

'Like I said, Cap,' said Hook, his voice laced with jealousy, 'you won the lottery.'

'What if they say no?' said Vine.

'Then we earn their trust,' said Tash. 'Or we just do it anyway. I could've done it now. I've only got to plug you in and flick a couple of switches.'

'You don't know that,' Vine cautioned.

'Of course I do. This is what I do, remember? If the Cynosure can't see how much use you would be then she's a fool.'

'And you don't believe that.'

Tash sighed as she shook her head. 'No I don't,' she admitted. 'I got so excited when I saw her. Do you think she noticed? I didn't make a fool out of myself did I?'

'Not at all,' said Vine, smirking. 'I'm sure she's had worse.'

'Shut up you! I can't help being a fan.'

'You could've been nicer to Gregor though.'

'Hey, that old man hasn't had his ego massaged in a long time. He's happy enough. I'm just planting a few seeds that'll grow later.'

'Careful,' Vine warned. 'You don't want this to backfire. To get Stella we'll need Gregor; she cares for him.'

'He's old news,' said Tash dismissively. 'I'll show Stella all the cool new toys and she'll wonder why she ever needed him around.' Tash paused for a moment, a look of delight passing over her face as she clasped her hands together. 'I can't believe I'm on first-name terms with the Cynosure!'

'First-name terms and a look into my deepest, darkest places,' said Stella. She smiled as she approached the desk. 'At least the bloody, gory bits of me.'

'Sorry!' Tash squeaked. 'I didn't know you were there.'

'That's okay,' said Stella, still smiling. 'That's the best time to hear people speak.' All three of them smiled, Tash just about covering her nervousness, before Stella continued. 'We're going to talk about Vine tomorrow,' she said. 'We want Jared's opinion and he's not up to it at the moment.'

'I hope he's okay,' said Tash.

Stella nodded. 'He's fine. Just needs some rest. So for now we can carry on if you're ready?'

'Of course!' said Tash, excitedly. 'I'm been looking forward to this for years. Let me show what I've done so far.' She directed Stella to the monitors to show her the readouts of data that would allow her to fix and even improve the augments in her legs, arms and torso.

Ben had counted another man. That meant five. He would watch for another few days just to be sure.

He was bored. The zombies that filled the space between him and the museum were completely unaware of his presence. That had to stay that way but there was nothing to stop him lining up a few shots on the other side of the building.

Grabbing his rifle, he headed to a rear window. A scattering of walking corpses dotted the road and there were bound to be more in the trees beyond. He took aim on a woman. She was wearing a jogging outfit, the sports brands still just about visible on her filthy, blood-stained vest and shorts. She was dark-haired, young. She had been for a run on her

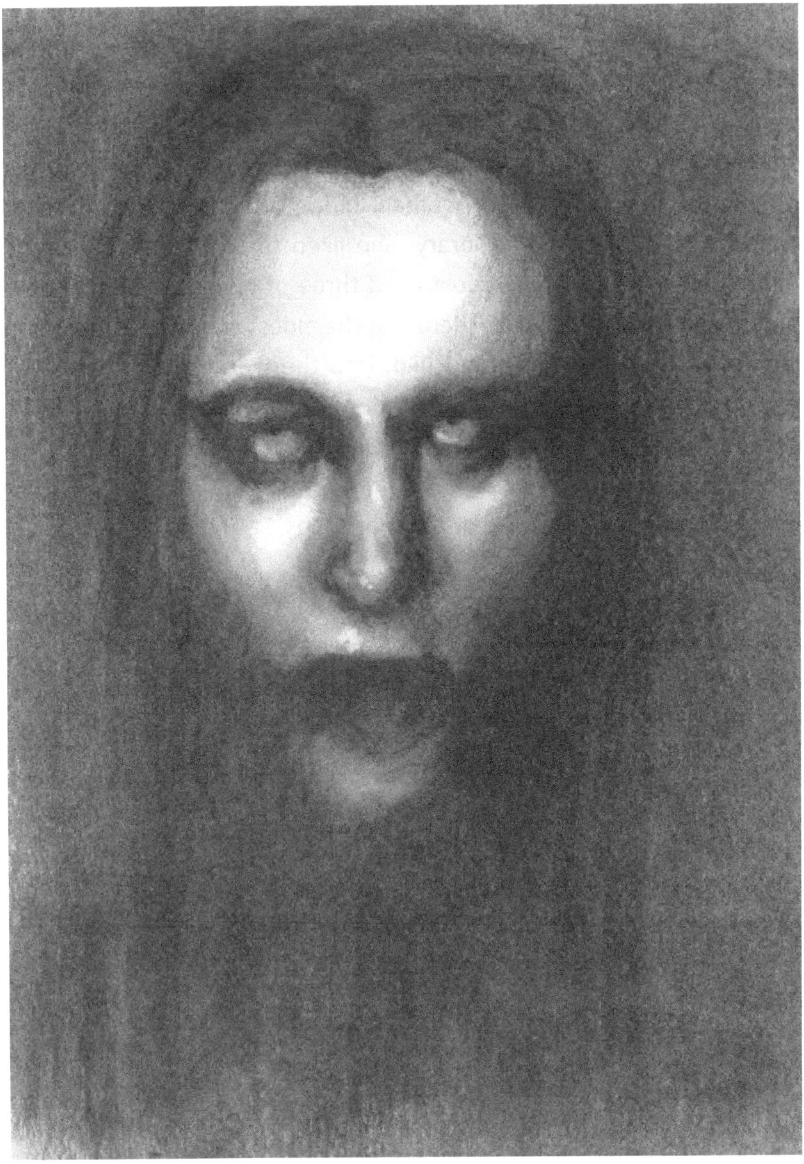

day off from working in the supermarket. She didn't have kids yet but she planned them with her boyfriend. They were due to get married next year. They'd agreed a house in the new housing partnerships that were springing up all over London. They would have kids soon after. She promised herself that she would still run even when she was pregnant. Ben shot her, dropping the zombie, collapsing the memories.

He switched to another woman, older, more conservative in her dress. She had been to the library. She liked to read. She'd never had children but a man she was seeing had three of his own. She had never found a way to get along with them and the eldest was expecting to bring their first child, their first grandchild, into the world by Christmas. She was wondering whether she wanted to keep seeing the man. The question had filled her time and distracted her from everything else. Ben shot her.

A dozen more targets, a dozen more lives, stumbled before him. He was the master of them all.

Early morning sunshine flooded the Victoria and Albert. Stella walked purposefully to the cafeteria to find Jared, slumped on a shallow padded sofa. The red of the plastic material was faded but bright and dust surged through the shafts of the light, bombing Jared with tiny particles.

'Get up and don't say that you're sorry,' said Stella. She stood over him, her right hand on her hip, her left arm still in its sling.

Jared jerked awake, saw Stella, a silhouette of expectation, and turned from her, burying his head into the space between the seat and the back of the plastic padding. His breath was suddenly loud, echoing, mournful.

'Up!' Stella repeated.

Jared shuffled over, squinting up. 'I'm...'

'Don't say it, because you aren't, not really. You regret it, I know that. You regret what you let yourself do. But you're not sorry. You can't be because you know that you'll do it again tomorrow.'

Jared slumped back, the plastic wheezing at the assault.

'So we need to make sure tomorrow never comes.' Stella softened her voice a little. 'And I know that it won't because if it does you'll let us down. You'll fail Hook, Gregor, Vine and Tash. You'll fail me.' She kneeled down to him. 'But the man who's spent three years out there won't let me down. That man survives and so do his friends.'

Jared shook his head. 'Not for long.'

'No one lives forever.' She nodded at the sling supporting her left arm. 'No one's invulnerable. No one gets through this for even a day without help. That's what we do, Mr Jenks. You know it better than I do.' She leaned close to him. 'Get up. Get showered. Help us.'

He stared into her face and saw the determination etched into it. His head swam with pain and fear, like it always did, like it always had. Like he always had, he pushed it back down and readied himself to face the day.

He nodded to Stella.

She stood and reached her hand down to him, her fist pushing through the swirling dust and the pain and the fear. He grabbed it.

'What about Vine?' said Hook. He, Gregor, a showered Jared and Stella sat in the middle of the desk in the rotunda. The green and blue chandelier glittered above them.

'We need him on our side,' said Stella. 'Deny him this and we drive a wedge between us before we've even started.'

'Too much power for one metal man,' said Hook, shaking his head.

'I trust him,' said Gregor.

'You're biased,' said Jared. 'He saved you. You're seeing an angel, not a man with enough firepower to take out this whole building.'

'Just what can an angel do?' said Stella. 'We never saw them do anything much, other than fly and recharge. And the dead ones' lasers of course, but I never really paid that much attention to them before the crash.'

'Well,' said Jared. 'You were kind of busy. As for the angels, they're like you and Hook but much, much more. They're augmented with bio-mech tech but it's the robotic components, the things that make them cyborgs rather than just enhanced humans, that make them walking tanks. They fly, they're strong, they're fast and they're armed. Their lasers have four basic settings: stun, injure, kill and destroy.'

'What's the difference between kill and destroy?' said Hook, still determined to be unimpressed by Vine.

'You kill a living thing. You destroy non-living things.' Jared shrugged as if what he was saying was obvious. 'Vine could take out a building, stop a vehicle. I don't mean regular vehicles, I mean armoured transports, tanks, fighter jets, bombers. With a hundred angels, you could take a country. With a thousand you could take the world. That's why everyone had them. So that no one could control all of them.'

'What if one lot of angels wanted to fight another lot of angels?' said Hook.

'Safeties were built into the tech that the People gave us. Everyone wanted the angels and the weapons, so they all agreed to the limits. No angel can shoot at another angel. Ever. They can only fire on living things with the express permission of angel control. And I don't mean low-level operators like me. That was when the politicians would have to be involved.'

'Why have that permission at all?' said Gregor.

'Certain extreme situations,' Jared replied. 'Use your imagination. Regular crimes like hostage taking. Accidents that would require vehicles or buildings to be cut back to get at people. North Korea, the Middle East and the NUSA never wanted to join the rest of the world. What if they suddenly got interested?'

'We planned for war?' said Stella.

'We always plan for war,' said Jared. 'We plan for it so that we don't have to fight it.'

'So if Vine can't target the deads,' said Gregor, 'how come the dead angels can target us?'

'I don't know,' said Jared. 'I've always assumed it's something to do with their own death and whatever it is that keeps their brains active on an instinctive level. The robotic parts of the dead angels must be acting on their own programming, and without a consciousness to interpret the reams of data they must see every living human as a threat.'

'But not the deads?' said Stella.

Jared shook his head. 'They're dead. They won't register on the angels' systems. They're just so much tumbleweed to them.'

'What about Vine?' said Gregor. 'If we flip his switch he can target the deads but will he be able to take on the Angels?'

Jared shook his head. 'No. Just the deads. I've no idea if that works both ways round. The angels' systems may register Vine as a threat and okay an attack out of instinct.'

'Even without that,' said Gregor, 'Jared's making him sound even more useful.'

'It's too much,' said Hook. 'Too much for one man.'

'The candidates for angels were carefully selected,' said Jared. 'Psychological profiling as well as physical compatibility. Not everyone that applied made it to the metal suit. We can be sure that Vine was well vetted.'

'And what psychological profiling has he had that makes up for three years trying to survive when he can't use his weapon? That'd be enough to drive anyone nuts.' Hook folded his arms as if he had won the argument.

Gregor was already shaking his head but Stella cut across before he could speak. 'We wait a week. We're locked down anyway, so it doesn't matter. We keep an eye on him and Tash and make the decision after we know them better.'

Reluctant nods greeted her suggestion.

As they all stood to leave, Stella called to Hook. 'Wait,' she said. 'Can I talk to you?'

Gregor and Jared glanced at them, the former busying himself with his equipment and the latter smiling as he headed off to the garden.

'I just wanted to say,' said Stella awkwardly, 'about what you did with the firebomb and the angel...' she paused. 'I know you'd do exactly the same again...' Hook was nodding furiously but Stella held up a hand to stop him from speaking, knowing that if she didn't say this now she never would. 'I just wanted to say good. It's good that you would do it again.' She reached up and patted his chest.

Hook was lost for words but his face shined. He reached up slowly to hold her hand but she pulled it away, turning from him to Gregor and taking a deep breath before nodding to the older man. 'Let's get started on these augments,' she said. 'We've got a lot to do.'

Hook smiled at the back of her head and headed off to follow Jared to the garden.

The days passed peacefully for the people in the Victoria and Albert Museum. Hook kept Jared busy in the garden, Gregor and Tash worked on Stella and Vine, upgrading and fixing the former and servicing the latter. Gregor's equipment had not seen so much use in years as Tash's cameras and innovative ideas pushed them forward.

Even with her arm in a sling, Stella still managed to join in with the simulations, making sure the augments were just right. She slammed into the Kistler Piezoelectric 3D Force Platform and ran for miles on the running machine, jogging, sprinting, jumping. She punched, she kicked, she head-butted. This was one of Tash's proudest moments as a skull augment along with angel alloys supporting her neck meant that Stella could use her forehead to hit with a force of 2000 lbs psi. That would be enough to crack a dead's skull and maybe even incapacitate it if the bone fragments went deep enough. But Tash and Stella were most pleased with the Cynosure's wings. They were back, the skin around her shoulders and upper arms raising and hardening to a titanium finish instantly, allowing her to barge anything out of the way. She would watch her shadow, her shoulders reforming into the horns of wings, like an angel's feathers tucked back, ready for flight. Or fight.

In testing Gregor and Tash simulated a crash with Stella and a vehicle moving at thirty miles per hour. Neither had come out of it well, but the bio-mechs were convinced that Stella would survive.

We'll test that one another time, Stella had said.

The two bio-mechs compensated for Stella's injury. Stella would throw the sling away when she was frustrated and use her augments to control her arm. She would only reluctantly replace the sling when the pain reminded her that an augment was just that, a thing to enhance her body, not replace parts of it.

Gregor was happier than he had been in a long time. He was useful, Stella was happy, Hook was busy, Jared was distracted just enough. All of them quickly became used to Vine's golden wings spread out in the garden to charge. They got used to it but they never got bored of watching it. Gregor was so happy that he almost forgot that none of it could last, that eventually they would have to deal with the deads and the angels again.

Ben grew bored and frustrated. He'd confirmed there were six people, well, five people and one cyborg and his listening device had revealed some very interesting information. He had hardly been able to stop himself from running straight to Kyle with the news, but he had confirmed it first. The Cynosure was there. Stella the Killer. He had told Kyle and the boss was as excited as him. Wait, he'd said. Wait and watch. But it was hard; the Cynosure's presence was driving Ben to distraction.

He left the spying equipment and headed for the back of the Ismaili Building. Outside the window dozens of corpses littered the road but there were still a few of them on their feet, shuffling blindly. Ben raised his rifle. Allowing his thumb to slide to the power switch, he moved the lever smoothly to its highest setting and aimed at the farthest zombie. It was a man, an old checked shirt hung raggedly from its frame and drool dripped from its beard. He worked in a game shop, had tattoos up and down each arm. No kids, never any plans for any. Spent his evenings online looking at things that he would be embarrassed to admit to. Ben pulled the trigger. A much larger bolt of energy burst forth, the fizzing sound of the discharge loud enough to make the nearest zombie glance his way. The bolt slammed into the zombie's torso, obliterating it in a shower of checked shirt and tattooed gore. The zombies nearby looked to the sound of the wet explosion and stumbled towards it. Ben switched to another target, destroyed it, then another and another, his weapon warming his shoulder and inner arm.

He stopped and threw open the top of the rifle to expose its solar cells to the sun. Smiling, he leaned against the window frame and waited.

Stella stepped from the shower. Her final augment was in place, a simple but vital component in her spine. It would support her, make sure she didn't end up like Hook. He was next through the sims and on the table; his back was wrecked from supporting his enhanced frame. Angel tech would make sure that he didn't collapse in front of hungry deads.

She dried herself carefully so as not to disturb any of the fresh dressings expertly applied by Tash. Stella had to admit that the woman certainly knew what she was doing, maybe even more than Gregor. She tut-tutted at herself for what felt like traitorous thoughts against Gregor but she knew that the old bio-mech had fallen for Tash. She was the daughter that Stella could never be. The Cynosure laughed out loud at the thought and caught her reflection in the mirror. No bags under her eyes. No frown of aches and pains. She could get used to this.

The pills were in her room. So was the syringe.

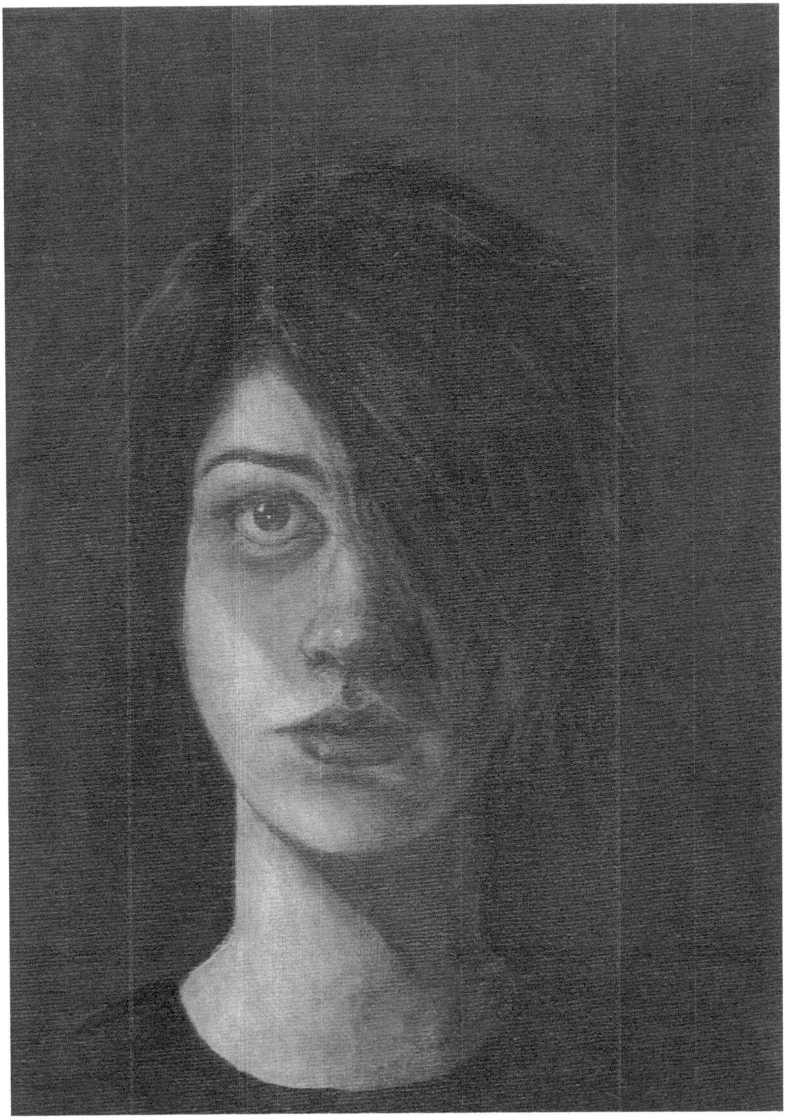

No aches, no pains. Not tired. Fresh, alert, ready.

Just another day, she told herself, maybe two and she wouldn't need them anymore.

Hook and Jared heard the whine of the jetpacks. They scanned the sky for the telltale signs of the Angels. Their view was framed by the buildings of Vic's and that limiter would mean that it would be hard for the Angels to detect them in the garden. Nevertheless they moved to the shadows of the buildings, keeping their movements slow and careful.

'There,' said Hook, pointing to a shadow as it flashed by, paying no attention to them but still slowing.

'And another.' Jared pointed. Two angels, both stopping nearby. That was not good. The two of them headed inside and dashed to the rotunda to find Gregor, Tash and Vine.

'Angels,' said Jared. The other three immediately stopped what they were doing. 'Where?' said Gregor.

'Stopping near the front. We'll go check.' Hook and Jared ran through the freezer rooms and pounded up the stairs, Tash and Vine close behind.

They arrived at the window just in time to see the last of the angels slowly disappearing behind the Ismaili Building.

'What do you suppose they're up to?' said Tash. She was still wearing the clean white t-shirts and bright red shoes.

Hook answered her. 'No idea. Where's Stella?'

'I'm here,' said Stella as she joined them. She was flushed, her face red as if she had done more than just run up a couple of flights of stairs.

'You okay?' said Hook.

Stella nodded. 'Never better. What's going on?'

'Angels,' said Jared. He nodded across the road. 'They're just behind that building. No idea what they've found.'

'Well it isn't us,' said Stella. She glanced down at the deads. They were agitated by the close proximity of the angels and noisier than usual as they shifted their attention from Vic's to the angels. It wouldn't last long now that the cyborgs were gone but perhaps this distraction could be used. 'Fancy going clubbing?' she said to Hook and Vine. The two men smiled.

Ben watched the angels land on the street behind the Ismaili Centre. He smiled as he relished the workout ahead. Putting the rifle on full power always attracted the angels. Checking the weapon, he noted that he had enough power for three high-energy blasts. More than enough to take out two angels.

Standing in full view at the window, he counted under his breath as he passed the after-shave bottle under his nose. It was usually about twenty seconds and he had never got past thirty-six. That was the record for how long it took an angel to notice him. He could never decide if that was a long time for a dead-headed robot to realise he was there.

Five, six, seven. The bottle swung beneath his nose, a scented pendulum slicing away the seconds. He replaced the lid when he got to twelve, screwing the top on tightly and replacing it in his pocket. Eighteen, nineteen, twenty, twenty-one, twent...

The nearest angel, turned to him, raised its arm and fired, the red beam arrowing towards him in a microsecond, the second only another microsecond behind that.

Ben was careful not to shout his excitement as he threw himself forwards and through the window frame, the two red beams shooting into the space behind him. Heart pounding with euphoria, Ben rolled to his feet, lifted his rifle and blasted the nearest angel, and rolling again before the bolt had even finished smashing the cyborg's chest plate, lifting the angel off its feet and ten metres back to slam into a tree.

Another red beam cut the air above him and he stopped his roll dead before the next shot flashed through the space where his roll would have taken him.

The remaining angel was too slow to react to Ben's change and failed to fire again as the high-energy bolt hit it full in the face, shattering its skull, neither metal nor bone able to resist the power.

Adrenaline coursed through his body. Ben smiled as he felt it run through him, charging his blood and electrifying his skin. It was as if his exhilaration had been given life and it were trying to escape his lean, muscular frame and dance beside him as another version of himself made of pure energy.

He raised his face to the sky, closing his eyes to focus on the thrill moving through him.

And then it was gone, like it always was, leaving him bathed in sweat and bliss.

He dropped his head back down and opened his eyes to see Craig staring at him.

'Wait,' said Vine as they moved through the freezer room. Everyone stopped, the hum of the freezers the only sound. 'Weapons fire. One shot, two, three,' he said it quickly, the shots faster than he could count, 'four, five...' he paused. 'They've stopped.'

'Is someone alive over there?' said Tash.

'Vine,' said Stella, 'get over there and check.'

'No,' said Tash. 'He can't fight angels.'

'Will they attack you?' said Stella.

Vine looked from one to the other. 'I don't know, I've always avoided them as much as I can. Whether they would or they wouldn't attack me, they may attack anyone I was attempting to rescue. I may be able to be quick enough to have a look, but Tash is right; I can't be quick enough to rescue anyone.'

'Any more shots?' Jared asked. Vine shook his head. 'Then there's no one to rescue.'

They stood in a circle, staring at each other, the knowledge of deaths so close by a shroud over their emotions.

Hook broke the spell. 'What do you want to do?'

Stella gave a grim nod. 'Let's see if we can thin the numbers.'

They passed through the rotunda, Hook and Vine grabbing their weapons, the spiked mace for Hook and Vine his whale bone.

'You're not thinking of going out there?' said Gregor to Stella. 'It's too risky with your arm.'

'I know,' said Stella. 'But I can hold a door open. Jared, you get the other door. We'll let the meatheads have all the fun on this one.'

'Facing up to a few hundred deads with nothing but a pointy ball on a stick?' said Hood. 'Not exactly my idea of fun.'

'You okay?' said Tash to Vine. The huge man nodded in return and smiled at her, before he moved to the solid wooden doors. He took the left, while Hook went right.

Stella and Jared moved ahead of Hook and Vine and put their hands on the bars that sat across each of the doors. 'We keep these doors open,' said Stella. She stood next to Hook while Jared was there to support Vine. 'As soon as it gets too much fall back into here and we'll slam the doors. Make sure you come back in at the same time so that neither of you get surrounded.' She gave Hook a hard stare. 'That means talking to each other and working together. Got it?'

'Got it, boss,' said Hook.

Vine nodded and twisted the grip on his whale bone, levelling the pointed end like a lance.

Tash and Gregor stood back, both worried but the older bio-mech covering it with a scowl while the younger tried to smile again at Vine.

'Ready?' said Stella. 'On three, Jared.' The captain nodded back. 'One, two, three!' They both hauled up the bars and dragged the door open.

'Oh no,' said Tash. Her voice was a loud whisper, the volume of her words taken away by the sight of deads, their backs to her, filling the limited vista offered by the doorways. 'There's too many.' She added.

'They'll be fine,' said Gregor.

Hook and Vine surged through the wooden frames, Vine's lance skewering the back of a dead's head immediately and Hook swinging his mace and smashing the skull of another. Within seconds there were six new corpses on the floor and Hook was still swinging while Vine had spun his bone around and was clubbing dead after dead, dropping them to their knees and kicking them over.

Stella held her position in the doorway, itching to join the two men and silently cursing her arm. She watched as Hook and Vine stood shoulder-to-shoulder, smashing the deads even as their bodies turned towards them. Quickly, there was a wall of deads and Hook's reach was limited compared to his cyborg companion. He stepped forward to brain another dead, another step, another swing of the mace.

'Hook!' Vine called as he continued to jab and swing with his longer weapon. 'Stay level with me!'

'Listen to him, Hook,' Stella called.

Hook stepped back down from the deads' corpses. 'I can't reach,' he said.

The horde of deads had turned back to Vic's and they pressed forward as one mass, falling and tumbling over the corpses of the deads already put down. Hook had to dance back out of the way as clawed hands reached for him. He swung wildly, the spikes on his mace catching fingers and tearing them off in spouts of blood, but he missed the skulls.

'That's it!' Stella shouted. 'We're done. Get back!'

Vine glanced over at Hook and the two men retreated together, the deads still falling and tripping towards them like a tsunami of rotten flesh.

'Inside!' Stella and Jared shouted together.

Tash dashed forward, Gregor too slow to stop her. 'Vine!' she cried out, rushing to Jared's side.

'Get back,' Jared grunted at her, shoving her with his elbow.

Vine and Hook backed in through the door frames, the former still using his superior reach to jab at the deads, while Hook fell through into the safety of Vic's and Stella slammed the door closed just as the deads were rising to their feet once again. Vine was just a couple of seconds behind him and Jared slammed the door. He and Stella let the bars fall back into place just as the crush of deads hit the wood. It held, the noise of their pressure the only sign of their presence.

The heavy breaths of five people filled the space just inside the main entrance to Vic's. 'Maybe,' said Stella between gasps. 'That wasn't such a good idea.'

'Back to the thumpers,' Hook agreed.

'Will the doors hold?' said Tash.

'No problem,' said Gregor.

And then the doors exploded.

Ben watched through the lens of the camera as the dust and smoke cleared. The zombies were surging through the shattered doorways into the museum. He couldn't see the people inside, couldn't see their faces. He needed to see their fear. He stepped onto the body of Craig, the man's head was pushed sideways against the floor, his eyes staring at nothing, and stepped onto the window frame to gain the elevation he needed.

There. A live one. It was Tash. He zoomed in on her. Her face was streaked with blood and the zombies hadn't even reached her yet. Her face was a mask of bloody anguish as she tried to reach forward but an old man held her back, shouting silently, desperately over her shoulder.

Ben smiled as he made his gift for Kyle.

They had all been knocked off their feet, even Vine, and were covered in great jagged splinters of hard wood. Stella looked about her, assessing the others as quickly as she could. Vine was already rising to his feet, Tash had a cut across her forehead that was sending streams of blood down her face, Gregor was moving towards her, limping badly, Hook was struggling to his feet, one of his arms covered in red ribbons of blood. Jared was nowhere to be seen.

She tried to remember where Jared had been standing but it was no use. Confusion was the only thing she knew, her own senses still numbed from the blast. She realised that she was covered in wooden debris and started to extricate herself, checking for injuries at the same time. As far as she could tell, even though her arm hurt like hell, she was okay.

'Where's Jared?' she shouted to the others.

Hook blundered to his feet. 'Get back, Stella!' he cried.

She looked over her shoulders; the deads, blown back by the initial explosion, were streaming to the ruined doorway and the first were already falling through. Jared was on the floor, trying to get up, trying to run.

Hook dashed forward, ignoring Vine's cry telling him to wait and smashed into the first few deads, swinging his mace to smash them away from Stella. He grabbed Jared under one of his arms and hauled him away.

Vine ran forward to join Hook. Tash made to run after him but this time Gregor caught her and held firm through her anguished screams for Vine.

Stella moved behind Hook, kneeling to Jared. 'C'mon,' she said to Hook. 'We need to get out of here.'

'Get back,' he said to her. 'I can hold them off.' He swung at another dead, the spikes of his mace piercing its skull and ripping pieces of brain and bone away in a shower of gore.

'Jared?' she shouted. The captain's face was blank, like he wasn't there. 'Can you stand, Jared?' Still nothing. 'C'mon, Captain. On your feet!'

Then Vine was there, clubbing the deads with efficient blows. 'We can't hold them. Not for long.'

'We can,' said Hook. 'We hit them one at a time and they fall down. We keep hitting, they keep falling.'

Vine smashed another two skulls before replying. 'We must fall back. We'll be surrounded. Start moving backwards now and Stella can help Jared.'

Hook looked over to the angel, ready to argue, but he knew that he was right. He nodded, turned back to the deads and swiped at another dead face, taking the front half of its head clean off.

'Stella,' said Vine. 'Start dragging Jared back towards the freezer room. We can maybe make a stand on the stairway.'

Stella nodded and hooked her one good arm under Jared's armpit and started dragging. He was heavy, it would have been easy if she had both arms. She gasped in frustration as she hauled him backwards and further into Vic's.

Hook huffed and puffed through the carnage, suddenly pleased there was a plan. The deads were beginning to circle them, vultures attentive to their fatigue. 'Can we speed it up?' he yelled to Stella.

'I'm struggling!' Stella replied. Then Gregor was at her side and Tash as well, grabbing and pulling at Jared. Stella could see that Tash was crying, the blood, still fresh on her forehead but watered streaks on her cheeks. Stella nodded at her as they lifted together and she returned the gesture, determined not to fail. They lifted together and picked up the pace, shouting at Jared all the while.

Suddenly Jared shook his head and saw what was going on around him. Vine and Hook above him, fighting, the rest behind him, pulling. 'I'm okay!' he shouted. 'I'm okay. Let me up. Let's get out of here!'

Stella, Gregor and Tash pulled him to his feet. He staggered for a moment then steadied himself.

Hook turned to see, twisting his back as he did so. He yelled in pain, snapping every dead head in his direction to watch as he fell, clutching his back with one hand and feebly waving the mace with the other. As he crashed to the floor, Stella turned to him. She saw the deads crash down onto him, the clawed hands clutch at him, the mouths fall on him.

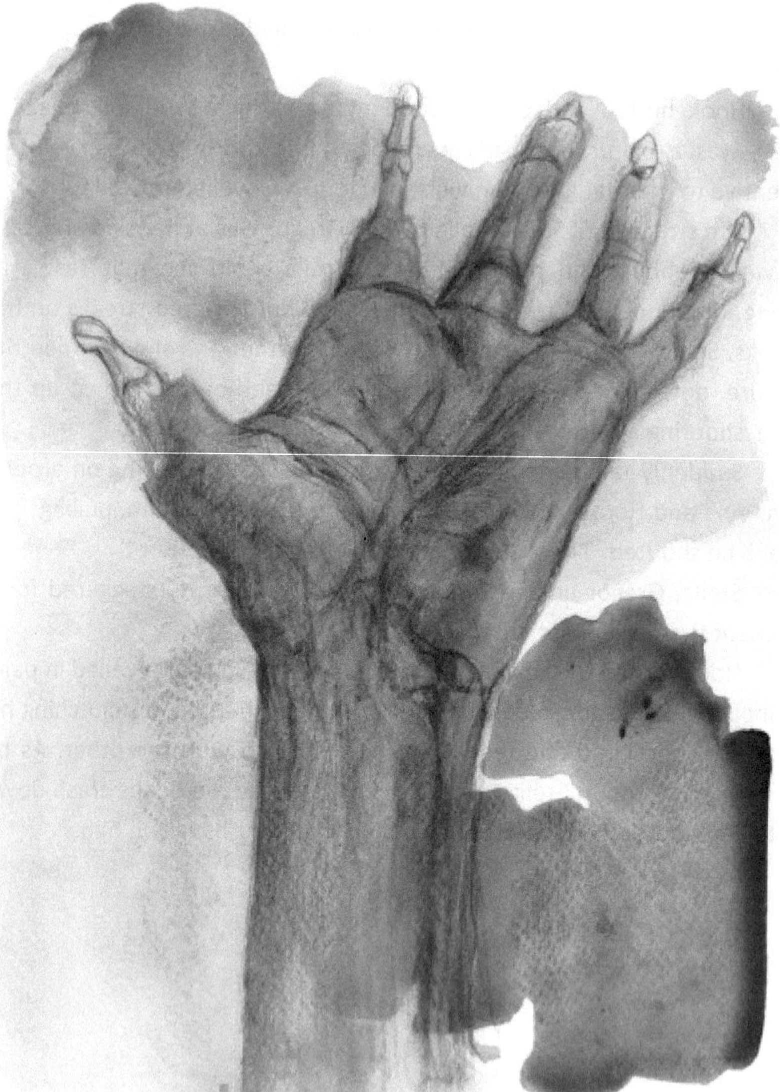

She ran forward, cutting off Vine and pulling her arm from the sling. Ignoring the pain, she activated her wings, flaring her shoulders as she crashed into the deads, scattering them from Hook. She rolled to her feet, stifling a cry of pain from her arm and set to the deads with her bladed feet, slashing and stabbing them back and away from Hook.

Vine stooped to grab the big man from the floor and slung him over his shoulder, staggered for a moment under the weight and then pushed on.

'Stella!' Gregor yelled. 'We've got to go!'

Stella turned back to them, pain and frustration twisting her face into a grimace. She looked to the prone form of Hook over Vine's shoulder and saw the blood pouring in ribbons down both of his swinging arms. Saw the bite in his shoulder, a huge rent in his flesh that revealed the titanium beneath.

They moved further in to the museum, into the rotunda beneath the blue and green chandelier, its dancing shards of light mocking their escape.

Stella ran after them, leaving dead fingers clawing and grasping at thin air. 'Wait!' she yelled. 'Put him down. Put Hook down.'

Vine lowered Hook to the desk just as Stella caught up. She looked down on Hook, concern in her eyes.

'Stella?' said Gregor. 'We have to go!'

Stella looked at Hook and to the deads passing into the museum. She watched them shuffle closer. Knew that they had a minute at the most. She looked back to Hook and bent down to whisper in his ear. 'What do you want me to do?'

He rolled his head towards her. 'Survive,' he said, his voice cracking with pain. 'I want you to survive.'

Ben laughed out loud, the camera held out in front of him to record the scene. There she was! The Killer on his little screen. He zoomed in on her face; she looked so sad. C'mon, Killer, Ben thought to himself. He didn't say it out loud. No need for Kyle to know everything. But he giggled with barely suppressed excitement. He mouthed the words silently to himself: You've got to survive so that I can kill you.

Stella the Zombie Killer Part Twenty One

Stella stared down at the stricken Hook, tears of concern and regret forming at the corners of her eyes. The big man was breathing with little, hard gasps, fighting the pain to stare back up at her, his eyes alive with tears. He reached out his hand. She held it firmly and started to tell him that he would be okay.

She stopped, shaking her head at him and at herself for thinking of lying.

'Stella, we've got to go,' said Gregor. His hand was on her shoulder, gentle but urging her away.

'Go,' said Hook. 'Go and survive.'

Stella shook her head again and a tear broke free, falling onto Hook's cheek.

He smiled. 'That's nice,' he said. 'That's enough. You can leave me with that.' He tried to push at her hand but either his strength was gone or he didn't want her to go.

'Stella,' said Jared. 'Gregor's right. We have to go.'

The Cynosure looked to the mass of death stumbling through the rubble-strewn entrance hall towards them. The deads reached out as if they were calling to her, calling her home. Glancing back down at Hook, she whispered, 'I'm sorry,' and let go of his hand.

'We can't just leave him for them,' said Gregor. 'They'll tear him to pieces.'

'Vine,' said Stella, 'lift him again.'

'He's already dead!' Tash yelled. 'We've got to go!' Blood soaked her white t-shirt, the material splashed with a red so vivid and heavy it seemed as if it were still alive.

'I'm not leaving him to them,' said Stella, her voice calm and determined.

'Then put him out of his misery,' the other woman returned.

'That's not how we do things,' said Gregor. 'We're not killers.'

Tash turned to the benches and grabbed a long, thin screwdriver. She turned on Hook, raising the tool, ready to stab.

Stella stepped to her and grabbed her forearm, holding it firmly. She looked into Tash's eyes. Any attempt from Tash to stand up to Stella was short lived, the younger woman wilting under the Cynosure's gaze.

'He's dead already,' Tash hissed. 'We stay here and all we do is die with him.'

'We save who we can,' said Stella, her voice stony.

'You can't save him! He's got hours left at the most.'

'Then we save him for those hours!'

'Can we just go?' said Gregor, his voice harsh and desperate. He was looking at the deads, just seconds away.

Stella looked to Vine. Silently, she begged the angel to lift Hook, to take him with them, to give him those last few hours.

Vine looked to Tash and Stella turned away, looking back down at Hook and blinking to clear the sudden tears. She reached for Hook, tried to put her hands under him but the pain in her arm was bright and sharp, the bones within chafing like broken glass. She gasped at the pain and looked down into his eyes. I'm sorry, she mouthed.

Hook held his hand up to her, started to form the word go but Tash interrupted him.

'Just do it,' she screamed at Vine. 'Kill them all!'

The angel turned on the deads, his movements smooth and fluid even in his enormous armour. His electronic blue eye turned red as he raised his right arm. He paused for a split second, his head jerking up and down the front row of the deads just two metres from them. A red beam, thin and deadly, sprang from his arm, hitting the deads closest to them in the forehead and then moving on, slicing open the heads of those either side, making them drop like a row of dead flowers whipped with a cane.

'What the...' Stella started to speak and stopped as Vine lowered his arm.

The rest of the deads continued to press forwards, some stumbling over those fallen in front of them, others already clearing the bodies so that they were close enough to reach.

Vine snapped his arm up again, slicing neatly and carefully along the line of deads.

'He can't keep firing. He has to stop between shots,' Tash explained. 'If he doesn't, he'll attract more angels.' She was shouting as if the noise of the deads' approach was deafening or Vine's silent laser was somehow drowning out her voice. But the massacre was almost silent, just the sound of the deads' shuffling feet and their mournful groans across the rotunda.

Stella, Gregor and Jared nodded. Even Hook had raised his head to watch.

'Hell of a toaster,' he said through gritted teeth.

Stella laughed. She laughed long and loud as Vine sliced each row of deads, reaping his bloody harvest.

'Get back,' said Vine to the rest. 'I can mop up whatever's left, but without the doors, we could have a stream of them all night. The rest of you take Hook and I'll make a wall of the bodies to keep the rest of them out.'

Gregor moved to Stella to help her put her left arm back in the sling. She nodded gratefully while she watched Jared and Tash try to lift Hook.

It was useless. The big man was too heavy and his wounds meant that he could barely raise his head. His deathly pale face was drenched with sweat and the torn flesh at his shoulder was a purple so brilliant that it looked as if it could sustain life rather than take it.

The bite was acting quickly. Hook would turn soon. No hours left to save him for.

'Help Vine,' she said to the others, but never taking her eyes off Hook. 'I'll stay with him.'

Jared and Tash turned to her, concern and regret in both of their eyes. Quickly, Tash turned from Stella, the guilt obvious as she laid the screwdriver on the table before heading away, while Jared simply nodded, knowing that there was nothing else to be done.

Vine levelled another row of deads. The pressure of the walking corpses lessened with each swipe from Vine's laser as the bodies piled high. The angel was able to move forward and start to cull those outside of the museum.

Jared and Gregor darted forward to begin dragging the bodies into a semblance of a wall and quickly created a bank of cadavers around Vine.

Stella turned back to Hook. She took up his hand again and stared down at him. 'I always said you were a meathead,' she said. 'And now you're too heavy to move.'

'Nothing but meat, boss,' he said, raising a smile that quickly faded.

'I'm not your boss.' She said the words mechanically, knowing that Hook would want to play it out. 'I'm no one's boss. Can't even boss myself.' She sniffed back tears as she forced the words out of her reluctant mouth.

Hook gripped her hand more tightly as a wave of pain passed through his body. He shuddered and broke out into fresh sweats.

'You still smell like a pig,' said Stella. She smiled down at him. 'Still not looking after yourself properly. You'll never get a girl, smelling like that.'

'Had one for years,' he replied. He drew up his other hand and enclosed hers in a double clasp.

'You're not the last man on Earth,' said Stella. 'Not yet.'

He looked at her and laughed. 'Kill the other three and give me a kiss.' He laughed again as he said it. But the mirth quickly turned to pain and he had to rush the final words.

Stella laughed, fresh tears forming in her eyes as she did so. She reached her left hand to his double clasp and held his hopes and fears in a painful grip.

'Someone blew up our doors,' she said. 'I bet that was a man. A woman'd be too sensible to blow up perfectly good doors.'

'Get out there and kill him too!' Hook coughed and gasped through the words. 'You'd best not be long though.'

'Don't worry,' said Stella, her voice suddenly serious. 'I'll find him and I'll kill him.'

Hook patted her hand, the effort to do so enormous. 'Don't hate, Stella. Not for me.' He coughed, suddenly and violently. Stella could feel the heat coming from him as she tried to steady his huge frame.

She withdrew her right hand and looked to the others; they were dragging bodies and piling them on top of each other, using them as flesh bricks. Vine had switched back to his huge whale bone, reaching across the barrier and stabbing heads of deads who got close enough. Whenever he had the space he would reach over and grab another corpse to drag on top.

'You're going to be okay,' said Stella to Hook. 'Everything's going to be fine. We'll get the doors fixed; Vine can clear the rest of the deads while we do it. We'll get your back sorted so that you can come back out with me when we run low on important things.'

'Some new DVDs,' said Hook, his voice distant.

Stella nodded. 'Some action movies. A Van Damme box set.'

'Now you're talking.'

'And we'll find a pig from somewhere. We'll go out into the countryside and find two of them.'

'And clean the chickens.'

'And clean the chickens.' While she spoke, Stella reached for the screwdriver left on the table by Tash. 'The garden'll feed us so that we don't need so much power for the freezers.'

'We could hook up a games console.'

Nodding her head, Stella fought back tears that threatened to break her. 'A console with those fighting games.'

'There's a trophy that unlocks the Cynosure.'

She nodded again. 'I wore the motion capture suit for it. Just a couple of months before the crash.'

'What was it like?'

'Weird. Green screen and wires.'

'I was in the Cynosure Games expansion pack.' Hook grunted a painful laugh. 'Never got into the main game.'

Stella moved the screwdriver behind his head, its thin point aimed at the middle of his skull.

'I don't want you to do it, Stella,' he said, his voice suddenly mournful. 'I don't want it to be you.'

She froze, the screwdriver an icicle in her hand. 'You don't want to get up again, Hook. You don't want that.'

He looked into her eyes, tears swimming in the depths of his own and leaking trails across his cheeks, making lines in the blood and the dirt. 'I just don't want it to be you.'

The screwdriver fell back to the table and Stella's tears flowed. She wiped at her face with hand, sniffing back the tears but they rolled down her cheeks and dripped from the end of her nose onto Hook.

'And don't let the toaster do it. And keep Gregor away from me. Let the captain do it...' his voice faded and he had to breathe deeply before continuing. 'He'll be quick.'

Stella leant closer, her face within centimetres of Hook's. His eyes lit up with hope and she moved closer still so that her lips could brush against his. She kissed him tenderly, lovingly, and as she pulled away he sighed with contentment, smiling so widely that he looked like a child ready to go home.

And then she was gone, leaving him alone while she went to Jared to ask him to do what she could not.

Stella the Zombie Killer Part twenty Two

Passing the aftershave bottle back and forth beneath his nose, Ben inhaled deeply. His breathing was heavy and fast, the bottle moving quickly, a small splash of the fluid visible in the flesh between thumb and forefinger. He stared at the living angel as he cleared the zombies with passes of his laser. Held casually at chest height, the camera recorded it all but Ben needed to witness this with his own eyes as heads were sliced over and over again. Flicking his eyes back to the white-armoured figure, he saw an angel of death, a grim reaper taking its harvest. Suddenly the angel stopped, bent low and rose again, a huge staff in his hands. He began stabbing at the zombies' heads, dropping them more slowly but just as efficiently

Ben needed to see more. Needed to see suffering. He lifted the camera high and used the zoom function to glide the image past the angel and through the shattered doorway to the people beyond. Tash and two other men were moving to help pile the zombies.

Where was she?

There!

The Killer. Her face was wet with tears as she bent over the big man. The bitten. Ben's breathing quickened again. He had seen him fall, seen the zombies crash onto him, bite him. The turn. It could be quick. Ben enjoyed the turn. He looked down at the body of Craig beneath his boots. As he looked back to the museum, the Killer reached for something, Ben couldn't tell what, and held it behind the man's head. Ben held the camera as still as he could, waiting for the whatever it was to plunge into the skull. It didn't happen. The Killer bent to the bitten, kissed him. Ben watched, his lip curling in distaste as the killer walked away, grabbed the younger of the two men's shoulders and spoke to him, wiping at her eyes the whole time.

Ben spoke silently to himself, his voice a whispered whistle in the neck of the aftershave bottle. 'If you leak, you're weak,' he said silently to himself. 'Your eyes leak, Killer. I know that you're weak. I'm coming to get you, Killer. Not today. You're weak today. But maybe tomorrow.'

He licked his lips and held the camera steady.

'Now?' said Jared to Stella. Over his shoulder, Vine continued to hack and haul at the deads. 'Right now?' The sound of the bone hitting deads' heads and their bodies being dragged onto the fleshy wall punctuated their conversation. 'Shouldn't we wait till he's dead?'

'He's suffering,' said Stella, wiping her eyes for the tenth time in the half-minute they had talked.

Jared shook his head. 'I'm sorry, Stella, but I won't kill anyone. I'm not starting that. We wait till he turns. Otherwise it's just...' he trailed off, leaving the word unsaid.

'How did you survive out there, Jared?' Stella was suddenly aggressive, leaning at the captain.

He backed away from her, instinctively feeling for his jaw, still sore a week after her wake-up punch. 'By not killing,' he said to her. 'By staying human when everyone else was turning savage. I saw them, Stella. The killers. They weren't living. They weren't even surviving. I always swore I wouldn't be a killer.'

'You're army.' Stella said it flatly as if it were illogical to make any kind of moral protest.

'That's different. That's war.'

'This is war!'

'No it's not. This is survival. This is what's left. I won't make it a battle ground.' He stood firm, facing her with grim determination.

Stella could see the nervousness in him but knew he wouldn't change his mind. In that moment she hated him for it. 'The only thing you're making is a fight with Hook when he gets up and tries to eat us. This is the way it is now, *Captain*.'

'Not for me.' Jared turned from Stella and grabbed a limb fallen from the wall.

Stella watched him push it up and back into the folds of rotten flesh and clothing. Grey gore dripped down his arm as he did it. She looked to Gregor but the old man shook his head at her and carried on pulling another corpse onto the top of the wall.

Vine turned to her. 'Stay with him to the end,' he said. 'And then I'll do it before he turns.'

Tash nodded her head, as if in support of the angel.

Stella glared at Vine, at them all as if they had betrayed her. 'I can't...' She started but stopped, the eyes of the others suddenly spotlights, scaring her words away. She turned to Gregor. 'Be with him for me,' she said to the old man. 'I can't do it.'

Gregor gestured to the wall and to Stella's arm in its sling. 'Wall needs building, Stella. You're the only one who can be with him. And you're the only one he wants.'

She glared at the old man, trying to make her stare prove him wrong. Gregor couldn't return her stare but he didn't need to; her shoulders sagged as she accepted the truth.

Hook opened his eyes as she stood over him. Noticing that her warmth was gone, replaced by her usual cold distance, he smiled widely. 'There you are,' he whispered.

She moved closer to hear him, her movements stiff and awkward as she bent at her waist, keeping her back straight, one arm firmly at her side and the other making the sling a shield across her chest.

'There was someone who looked just like you here a few minutes ago. But it couldn't have been you. Too nice.' He smiled again, trying not to laugh at himself, trying not to shake with the pain in his back and shoulders.

Stella deliberately avoided looking at the bite wound and saw instead the thick splinter sticking into his other shoulder. Blood seeped from the wound, slowly, carefully, as if it were saving its energy for something else. 'I didn't see that before,' she said.

'I've got so many holes,' Hook replied with sigh. 'I can forgive you missing one of them. Hurts like hell, though. Be nice to have a little sympathy.'

'I don't do sympathy.'

'No, you don't.' Hook paused while a spasm of pain passed through him. Stella could feel the heat radiating from his body. 'You should. You save them but you don't care about them.'

'I can't.' Stella stopped herself, straightened, moving away from the body of Hook and her own confession.

'You can. You do,' he said. 'I've seen it. It's why they'll follow you.' He gasped back another wave of pain.

Stella's hand moved awkwardly towards him then stopped. It was stuck in the space between them, suspended like a criminal in a gibbet.

Hook reached out to take her hand, wincing with the pain in his shoulder. Stella allowed him to hold it but didn't return the grip. 'They're scared of you,' he said to her. 'And they're scared for you.'

'Good,' said Stella. 'It's good that they're scared. Fear keeps us alive.'

'But it doesn't keep us living.'

'There's no difference.'

'If there wasn't, you wouldn't need those pills.'

Stella glared at Hook, her eyes flashing with shock and anger. 'That's different.'

Hook shook his head. 'No difference. You and Jared. Both the same.' His voice grew weaker with every sentence. 'But you're stronger. You can get yourself and him and all the rest through this.'

Stella nodded, her fingers twitching in his soft grip. 'Day by day.'

'More than that. Let them live. Let yourself live. Don't make them afraid of you. Don't make them cut you off. Save who you can. Including yourself.'

Hook's grip loosened in Stella's hand and she suddenly gripped tightly, ferociously. She watched Hook's eyelids flutter and droop as if he were just tired or drunk or hungover. She gripped his hand, silently urging him not to go.

'Does it hurt?' Ben whispered to the image on the tiny screen of his camera. His voice was no more than a breath. 'Can you feel pain like the rest of us?' He put the aftershave bottle down on the windowsill and let his hand fall to the hilt of the knife strapped to his hip. He caressed the handle lovingly and glanced down at the body of Craig. He smiled.

Turing back to the Killer, his smile slipped as the wall of zombies grew high enough so that he could no longer see her clearly. In the next moments she would disappear behind the barricade of corpses. He watched for as long as he could, watched her stare at the bitten.

And then she was gone, obscured by a body thrown in his way by the living angel. The limbs of the corpse wind-milled for a brief second and then slumped atop the pile, leaving nothing but a wall of flesh and a few zombies stumbling against it. Ben watched as one managed to find a foothold and started an ungainly scramble. Just as its head neared the top the long sharp weapon appeared, stabbed it in the face and left it to slither down onto the floor, tripping another zombie attracted by its actions. It struggled to its feet and stared up at the wall, as if it were unsure of what to do. It stood and stared, its head tilted back like it was in the front row of a cinema and the movie made no sense.

Ben dismissed the creature and stepped down from Craig's body, grinding his heel into the fingers of one hand and smiling as he felt the bones break. He switched off the camera and placed it to one side before kneeling down bedside the body. 'Well, Craig. Looks like it's just you and me.'

He moved to the window and retrieved the rifle. Opening its solar charge panel he moved through to the rear of the building and placed it on a window ledge in the afternoon sun. 'Tomorrow,' he said to it.

Walking back into the room containing Craig's body, he rubbed his hands together with gusto. 'We're going to have so much fun,' he said as he pulled a pair of pliers from his pocket. Bending over Craig's head, he pulled his mouth open and tapped at his teeth with the pliers. 'You might just be the highlight of my day.' He tapped in a rhythm, making a mockery of the Match of the Day theme tune. 'But the Killer is the winner.' He stopped tapping, opened the pliers and hovered over the right molar. Snatching it in the pliers' teeth he pulled at it, yanking it out in one smooth motion. 'He shoots. He scores!' Blood welled in the hole and stained the teeth to either side. Ben grabbed the next and pulled it free and then another and another, grunting with the effort.

Within minutes he had a pile of teeth on the floor next to him. His red, sweaty face was split by a wide grin. 'And now the other little piggies.' He reached over and grabbed the hand that he hadn't already trodden on. Holding the little finger first, he looked to Craig's dead face. 'This little piggy went to market,' he said in a sing-song voice before pulling the finger back and snapping it at the knuckle. He grabbed the next finger. 'This little piggy had roast beef.' He snapped the next. 'This little piggy had none.' Another finger broken. 'And this little piggy stayed home.' Ben paused as he held the forefinger. 'Do you know, I think I got it the wrong way round. I'm sorry about that, Craig, I really am.' He snapped the finger savagely, bending it and crushing it until every bone was broken and he could feel the fragments grinding together beneath the skin. 'Tell you what. To make up for it, I'll leave the thumb unbroken. How about that?'

Craig didn't respond.

'I'll take that as a yes,' said Ben happily. He took the knife from his hip and held the blade at the base of the thumb. 'This won't hurt a bit.' He sliced into the flesh, blood spilling but not flowing from the wound. He carried on through the bone and out the other side. He held up the thumb, inspecting it closely. Suddenly he ran it up the body's arm. 'And this little piggy went wee-wee-wee, all the way home!' Ben stuffed the thumb into Craig's toothless mouth, leaving just a little of the nail poking out over the lips. 'There,' he said, nodding to the corpse. 'And now we're ready. Don't worry. No rush. In your own time, Craig.'

Ben took the aftershave bottle and settled back to lean against a wall, passing the bottle beneath his nose and pulling the camera over to place it on his lap. He hit the playback button and settled to watch the Killer cry again and again.

When Hook finally stopped breathing, Stella, her eyes dry, left his side, nodding to Vine as she moved away.

The living angel moved to Hook's side and placed his right hand on the big man's left cheek. 'Goodbye,' he said.

Gregor and Jared and Tash moved closer, gathering around the angel to murmur their own goodbyes. Vine's hand left Hook's cheek and he pointed his arm up at the forehead before looking to Tash.

'Go ahead,' she said.

The flash of red was there and gone in a microsecond but it left a streak of red light in their vision that lasted for several more seconds. The neat hole on Hook's forehead and the passage bored by the laser made sure that he would not rise again.

Author's note

Thanks for reading.

Who is Kyle? Who was driving the truck? Who left the thumper in the garage? How does the mobile phone have a signal? How will Stella and Jared cope with their addictions? How will they all cope without Hook? Can they trust Tash and Vine? Will Ben get to meet with Stella face to face?

Rest assured that this isn't the end for Stella and her crew. To read on just search for Stella the Zombie Killer Volume Two.

For the latest news on Stella go to www.alistairwilkinsonauthor.co.uk or find Alistair Wilkinson Author on Facebook or follow @algy04 on Twitter.

And remember, the Cynosure continues to fight for you.